CALIFORNIA CROSSFIRE

"Let the lady go!" Morgan shouted.

"Mind your own business!" The man took one hand from the terror-stricken woman and threatened to draw. "Ease off, stranger, and stay alive."

Morgan took one more step toward the man, whose hand darted for leather and drew a .44 out of his holster.

With an arcing movement of his right arm, back and up, Morgan brought the blacksnake whip into action.

The whip tore a bloody trail across the other man's hand. The gun dropped to the street. He howled with pain, let go of the woman, and grabbed his injured hand.

With a flick of his wrist, Morgan recoiled the whip. "Now what the hell were you saying, tough guy?"

Also in the *Buckskin* Series:

BUCKSKIN #1: RIFLE RIVER
BUCKSKIN #2: GUNSTOCK
BUCKSKIN #3: PISTOLTOWN
BUCKSKIN #4: COLT CREEK
BUCKSKIN #5: GUNSIGHT GAP
BUCKSKIN #6: TRIGGER SPRING
BUCKSKIN #7: CARTRIDGE COAST
BUCKSKIN #8: HANGFIRE HILL
BUCKSKIN #9: CROSSFIRE COUNTRY
BUCKSKIN #10: BOLT-ACTION
BUCKSKIN #11: TRIGGER GUARD
BUCKSKIN #12: RECOIL
BUCKSKIN #13: GUNPOINT
BUCKSKIN #14: LEVER ACTION
BUCKSKIN #15: SCATTERGUN
BUCKSKIN #16: WINCHESTER VALLEY
BUCKSKIN #17: GUNSMOKE GORGE
BUCKSKIN #18: REMINGTON RIDGE
BUCKSKIN #20: PISTOL GRIP
BUCKSKIN #21: PEACEMAKER PASS
BUCKSKIN #22: SILVER CITY CARBINE
BUCKSKIN #23: CALIFORNIA CROSSFIRE
BUCKSKIN #24: COLT CROSSING
BUCKSKIN #25: POWDER CHARGE

BUCKSKIN #23

CALIFORNIA CROSSFIRE

KIT DALTON

LEISURE BOOKS NEW YORK CITY

Special acknowledgment to Madelyn Tabler
and Mae Miner without whose help this
book would never have been written.

A LEISURE BOOK®

February 2005

Published by

Dorchester Publishing Co., Inc.
200 Madison Avenue
New York, NY 10016

ISBN 0-8439-2674-0

Visit us on the web at www.dorchesterpub.com.

1

Screams ripped the summer air and drowned out even the sound of the big Concord team's two dozen hooves hitting the packed dirt of the street. The screams reverberated over the stage's wheels, grinding to a stop.

Lee Morgan stepped from the coach and lifted his gear down from overhead, a tattered carpet bag and his black snake whip.

A man's voice commanded, "Come 'ere, bitch! You ain't goin' nowhere."

Another scream split the air.

What the hell's going on in this place? Morgan wondered.

He had no chance to glance around the dusty little town of Lost Canyon before he heard the woman cry out again.

She screamed over and over, long frightened wails, then screeched in desperation. "Help! Someone help me." Another scream, then, "Let me go! Won't anybody help me?"

Morgan spun toward the sound and saw the slender creature in the grasp of a great hulk of a man. Stringy dark hair hung long and lank from under his dirty hat. His arms bulged like hams out of his rolled-up sleeves. His massive hands held the woman by her upper arms and shook her.

Morgan couldn't hear at that distance what
the man said to her. It was hard to figure what
he was trying to make her do, or perhaps tell
her, there in the center of town.

Not many people were around, but the place
was by no means deserted while this scene
played out. A woman in a bonnet carrying a
basket on her arm turned to look. Some men
lounged against the front wall of the hardware
store. No one moved to help the woman.
Morgan wondered where the sheriff was. No
one lifted a hand.

The woman was young, beautiful, Morgan
could see from where he stood. Her auburn hair
was pulled together into a cluster of ringlets at
the nape of her neck. Wisps of curls escaped
around her face. She wore a long blue print
dress with lace at the sleeves and hem. It was
tucked in at her tiny waist.

Morgan dropped his gear at the edge of the
boardwalk and uncoiled the black snake whip,
his right hand behind him. The tied-down Bisley
Colts on his hips would be of no use to him right
now; he couldn't take a chance on hitting the
woman struggling in the brute's grasp.

Trailing the black snake whip, he took a step
or two in the direction of the big man and his
captive.

When the woman stopped screaming long
enough to take a breath, Morgan called out,
"That your husband, Missus?"

"No!" She sounded a cry of revulsion at such
a thought. "No. No!"

Morgan took a couple more steps toward the
two and warned, in a deadly level voice, "Let the
lady go, Mister. Now!"

The victim's dark eyes were wide with terror

and pleading as she turned her face toward Morgan. His heartbeat accelerated just looking at her. It would sure as hell take a whole posse of men, even bigger than that one, to keep Morgan from helping this enchanting female.

"Mind your own fuckin' business." The man released one hand from the terror stricken woman and threatened to draw. "Ease off, stranger, and stay alive."

Morgan heard squeals of fright from some other women, apparently seeing the threat of gunplay as they boarded the stage behind him.

He took one more step toward the man whose hand darted for leather and drew a forty-four out of its holster.

With an arcing movement of his right arm, back and up, which bystanders might have been led to believe was raising in an attitude of surrender, Morgan brought the black snake whip into action.

He heard the stage start off. He heard the crack of the black snake, and the report as the other man's forty-four discharged.

"Ahhhh!" It was like a cheer from several people on the boardwalk lining the street.

By the time the weapon fired, it was pointing toward the ground with the whip tearing a bloody trail across the back of his gun hand. The gun dropped to the street. He howled with pain, let go of the woman, and grabbed his injured hand.

With a flick of his wrist, Morgan recoiled the whip. "Now what the hell were you saying, tough guy?"

"I'll get you, you son of a bitch." The man's face contorted in fury. "You haven't heard the last of Brant Corson."

Morgan went closer. "That may be, but this lady better have heard the last of you."

Brant Corson started for the gun lying in the dirt. Morgan moved into his path and bumped the larger man with his shoulder. Corson swung a left. Morgan ducked, nudging the forty-four aside with the toe of his boot, and in turning gave Corson a left jab which bloodied his nose.

The big man snorted like a maddened bull and rushed at Morgan with both fists clasped and raised to hammer him into the ground. Morgan side-stepped, but not quite far enough. He took a glancing blow to his left shoulder.

In too close to use the black snake, Morgan dropped it and pounded his right fist into his enemy's mid-section. Corson grunted but his knuckles clipped Morgan below the eye. Morgan could feel the warm fluid start down his face and knew his adversary had drawn blood.

Regaining his balance in time, Morgan came back with a left uppercut to the giant's jutting jaw.

It stopped Corson long enough so that Morgan could kick the man's forty-four farther into the street.

Corson got his breath and came at Morgan again. The great bulk of the gargantuan figure could have crushed anyone he landed on, but Morgan, tall, lean and agile, was too fast for the heavier man. As Corson lunged, Morgan feinted and slid to one side, leaving only a booted foot in the man's way to trip him. Corson sprawled heavily in the dust cursing loudly.

Glancing around, Morgan found that the woman had completely disappeared. A pang of disappointment flicked through him. He wanted to see her, to know who she was, to make sure she was all right. He wanted to touch her, to know she was real. But she was gone, fleeing from the man she feared.

Since the lady was no longer in danger, Morgan swung around and retrieved his Stetson which had fallen to the ground. He slapped it against his leg to clear off the dust. Picking up his whip, he recoiled it, then gathered his carpetbag from where he'd dropped it and headed up the boardwalk toward a sign that said: Doubloon Saloon. Morgan glanced back once to make sure Corson, retrieving his firearm, was heading the other way.

Been in town about ten minutes and already made an enemy, Morgan thought.

He would not have been in this town at all, if he hadn't owed Hank Broom a big one. He had known Hank for years and they met now and again. Hank had a hair-trigger temper, which had given the two of them trouble more than once.

But Hank had also saved Lee Morgan's life, and it only took one of those to make Morgan obligated. So he was here in answer to his old friend's telegram. Besides, the way the wire read, it might be worth something, and if it turned out that way, he could use the money.

He took another look up and down the broad dusty street along which stood a couple of other saloons, a general store—General Emporium, the sign read—a hotel, and far down the other side a livery stable. He would check out the rest of the place when he found out why he was here.

He pushed through the swinging doors and walked into the Doubloon Saloon.

Morgan stood for a moment adjusting his eyes to the dimmer interior, then checked out the saloon's other customers. Not many were there in mid-afternoon on a weekday; a couple of men leaning on the bar about three-quarters of the way down, and three others arguing at a table at the far end of the room.

Hank Broom, the man Morgan had come to meet, stood talking to the rotund barkeep at the near end. Broom looked up as Morgan came in. " 'Bout time," he said.

Broom was half a head shorter than Morgan. His weatherbeaten face, below a bush of salt and pepper hair, wore a frown.

Morgan put down his gear and stuck out a hand. "Good to see you, Hank. What's it all about?"

"Draw him a beer," Hank told the barman. To Morgan he said in a lowered voice, "You didn't come here to rescue damsels in distress, Morgan. You were supposed to keep low."

"Hells bells, Broom, keep low? This town's so small people'd notice an extra flea on the local dog."

"Yeah, well . . . try not to put on any more theatrics."

The barman slid the beer across to Morgan and went on down the bar to wait on his other customers.

Broom and Morgan took their mugs over to one of the tables. Morgan dragged his gear along and dropped it on the floor beside his chair. The lead weighted grip on the two-foot long handle of the black snake hit the floor with a loud clunk. Morgan stuck out his foot and drew it in closer to him. The whip had saved his neck more than once both by lash and by using the handle as a cosh.

When the two men were settled at their table and had taken a couple of swallows of their beer, Morgan asked, "Now what's the big hush-hush proposition that got me to Lost Canyon?"

"We won't discuss it here," Broom told him. "Soon's we wet our whistle, we'll go down to the hotel and get you into a room. Then we can talk."

"Fine," Morgan said. "I hope it's worthwhile. I made the trip all the way from Denver to this place on California border. Lost Canyon, never even heard of the place. What there is of it."

Broom said. "It's okay in the summer. Don't want to stay around when winter comes, myself. I know this town from way back. In spring that dusty street out there is a river of mud from snow melting down from the mountains. Pretty hot in summer, but this is better than later, when you're either ass deep in the snow or can't get a grip on the ground for the ice."

"Never cared a hell of a lot for snow and ice, myself," Morgan agreed. "We gonna finish our business before summer is over? Only one person I might be interested in around here."

Broom snorted. "Never mind the women. But some interesting people go through here. And some of 'em never leave."

"Don't know as I want to be one of those, if you mean what it sounds like."

They finished their beer. Broom waved to the barman. "We'll be in again, Moe."

Morgan picked up his gear again and they strode down the street. A faint breeze rustled the big trees behind the buildings on the opposite side of the street. A boy and a dog tore past them and the boy suddenly came to a stop. He turned and stared at Morgan, his gaze transferring from Lee's face to his black snake whip. The youngster looked as if he wanted to say something, but changed his mind and ran on.

They reached the hotel, a recently painted white two-story building, which had a long veranda running the length of the front. The men went up the steps and across the porch making loud hollow sounds with their boots.

Hank Broom introduced Morgan to Jeb Rowe, and Morgan signed the register and paid for a room.

"I'm the owner along with my wife, Essie, here," the hotel man said, turning the book around to see Morgan's name.

"How long will you be with us?" the owner's wife inquired.

"Can't be sure, ma'am," Morgan told her and picked up his gear.

"Same thing your friend here said, a few days ago." She smiled. "If your room isn't all right, just tell us."

"Oughta be all right," he said. "Lucky number. Twenty-one. What are chances of gettin' a bath in this town?"

Essie nodded. "Just give us a little warning and we'll have Nelly fill the tub at the end of the hall on your floor. Twenty-five cents extra and the towel and soap are furnished."

"Thank you, ma'am. Hour or so from now'd do fine." He glanced at Broom to verify his time schedule. The shorter man shrugged.

Broom and Morgan went up the wide staircase to the second floor. "Where you located?" Morgan asked.

"Downstairs. Room six," Broom told him. As they stepped into Morgan's room and shut the door, he added. "Now we can have a talk. You ever hear of Hex Downs?"

"Downs? Don't think I ever knew anybody by that name personal, but seems to me I might've heard it sometime or other."

Broom glanced around the room. "You got the best room. Look at the size of it, and this one even has a fireplace."

"Well, since I don't plan to stay and wait for winter, I guess it don't matter if it has a fireplace or not." He took off his tan low-crowned hat, dusted the black band with the red diamonds against his forearm, and laid it on the bed. Then he methodically put his change of clothes into a bureau drawer, laid a couple of brushes on the dresser top, and washed his face in the basin with water from a large crockery pitcher.

"Hex was a train robber," Hank Broom said. "He was the one, in fact, who took care of stashing the loot. There were just two of them. One got shot dead during the robbery, and Downs took off to hide what part of the gold he managed to keep a hold on."

"Gold?" Morgan repeated.

"That's right. He likely got away with at least four ten-pound bars, a couple of 'em in each saddlebag."

Morgan whistled. "Just one of those would damn near pay a ranch hand's wages for ten years. Where is this fortune in gold bars?"

"The last place Downs was seen was here in Lost Canyon. In fact, he died in a gunfight right out there where you were putting on your little show earlier today."

"You think you know where the gold is
stashed. And you think we're going to find it."

"Have an idea how to find out where it could
be," Broom said. "Want your gun help."

Morgan went over to the lace-covered window
and brushed the curtain aside. The Sierra
Nevadas rose majestically in the far distance.
The lower slopes, covered with Ponderosa
pines, glinted green in the late afternoon sun.

He gazed down at the street where he had
scuffled with Brant Corson. He rubbed his left
shoulder. He could still feel where the massive
fists had hammered him. If the blow had landed
on his head, as intended, it could have broken
his neck.

He could almost see the woman with her
auburn hair, curly wisps blowing around her
face. He tried to imagine how her face would
look in serenity, or in passion, instead of terror.
He could visualize her long blue print dress
swirling around her ankles when Corson let her
go to draw his forty-four.

Morgan could feel a hunger in his lower belly
and between his thighs. He wished he could see
that auburn haired woman coming up the street
looking for him. But she was not out there.
Maybe he would be able to find her before he
was finished in Lost Canyon.

"So that's it," Broom said.

"Huh? Oh, sorry," Morgan mumbled.

"Thinking about that woman again?"

"What do we do to get this gold?"

Broom sighed. "Damn, I should have known
better than to ask *you* to come to a town where
there'd be any type of female. I should have told
you to meet me at some large boulder out there
at the bottom of the foothills."

"All right, tell me. I'm listening. What's the story?" Morgan let the curtain swing back over the window. He sat on the edge of the bed and faced Broom who had begun to pace the room. "Shoot."

"There's somebody else in town looking for the same gold we're after. That's one reason I wanted you along, in case there's trouble." He stopped pacing and sat in a chair beside the bed.

Broom took out his fixings and rolled a cigarette. When he had it lighted, he went on. "Hex Downs visited an old man who lives in a beat-up shack about eight or ten miles out of town. First thing tomorrow morning, we get a couple of horses. There's a livery right down the street. We go to see this old gent and find out what he knows."

"What are we going to do with this gold when we get it?" Morgan wanted to know. "Who did it belong to before Downs and his outfit came by it?"

"The U.S. Government. There's a reward . . . if we decide to tell 'em we've found it."

Morgan thought about that for a while. This would have suited his daddy to a tee, he thought. Sometimes his natural father, William Buckskin Leslie, fought on the side of the law and sometimes otherwise, but he always fought well and he usually fought fair. As long as he got his pay, he enjoyed it.

Frank Leslie's reputation was well known throughout the west. His fame fanned out from an Idaho ranch he'd finally settled down on about a half day's ride out of Boise. That was before he and Harve Logan had managed to kill each other with one simultaneous shot apiece.

Yes, Frank Leslie would have liked hunting for stashed gold. He'd have said something like, *Probably hell of a lot easier than panning for it.*

"Probably a hell of a lot easier than panning for it," Morgan said aloud. "You think this old gent we're going to see will be able to tell us something? If he knows, why doesn't he get it himself?"

"Can't say," Broom told him. "Maybe we'll find out in the morning. You gonna get something to eat before you turn in?"

"Soon's I find that bathtub," Morgan agreed.

He found the dressing room at the end of the hall. A buxom young woman, who told him her name was Nelly, poured two pails of steaming water into a tub in the middle of the room. A chair and two pegs on the wall served to hold the bather's clothes.

Morgan put his clean shirt and a change of socks and summer underpants over the back of the chair, hung his gun belt on it, and moved it closer to the bathtub. Then he sat down to take off his boots.

Nelly came in with another pail of hot water and a pail of cold water, and poured both into the tub. "That ought to be about right, Mr. Morgan. Usually is."

Morgan took off his shirt. "You plan to stay and scrub my back for me, Nelly?"

"That doesn't come with the price of the bath, Mr. Morgan." Nelly's cheeks were already rosy and when she blushed they got redder. But her eyes sparkled above her flirty smile as she left the room and shut the door behind her.

When he was clean and dressed, Morgan met Broom for their evening meal. The only cafe in town was apparently the best. Most of the tables were filled and only a few places were open at the counter. They took a couple of those and Broom recommended the stew. It was served with great chunks of hot sour dough bread and coffee.

"Coffee is great," Morgan told the counter maid.

"Have our own well. Deepest well in town and the best water in the west."

Later, after he and Hank Broom had finished eating and had ogled the counter maid some more, they stopped at one of the three saloons to toss down a brandy to cap off the day. They both managed to stay out of the brawls that broke out and back at the hotel, Lee Morgan made his way back to room twenty-one.

He brushed his low-crowned Stetson and laid it on the bureau, took off his gun belt and hung it on the straight chair within easy reach.

He was just about ready to strip down and get into bed when he heard a soft tapping at the door. "Yeah?" He drew the bolt and opened the door.

Before him stood the auburn haired woman.

This time she wore a soft gray dress, the bodice of it laced up and cupping her small breasts so that enticing white mounds showed above it. In her hand she carried a small carved leather grip, a one-of-a-kind satchel that had the look of something valuable. The bag was about a foot-long and eight-inches wide with two buckled straps around it.

Her dark eyes gazed up at Lee Morgan and she smiled tentatively. "May I come in?"

Morgan stepped back. He could scarcely trust himself to speak. She was even lovelier than he had thought.

"Yes," he finally managed. "That is, uh, certainly. Come in."

She brought an intoxicating scent in with her. Morgan closed the door and shoved the bolt quietly into place.

2

She moved like a cloud. Stepping into the room past him, she looked around her. "They seem to keep a nice hotel. It's a pleasant room."

Morgan nodded. He seldom encountered a woman, a lady, his mind amended, who left him feeling so like a schoolboy in short pants, so tongue-tied.

"I wanted to thank you in person," she said, turning to face him.

"You're welcome." He sounded like a school boy, to himself at any rate.

"You risked your life," she went on. "That man is a bully and a cold blooded killer."

"That's about the way I had him pegged," Morgan agreed. He didn't know whether to ask her to sit down or not. He liked the way she looked just standing there.

"I located you through Essie Rowe, downstairs." Her smile made the sunset seem insignificant. "I have found that Essie has a habit of knowing most everything. She saw the whole thing, the way you rescued me and all."

The gray dress she wore was soft, velvety, with a fitted top laced at the waist with silver cord. When she took a deep breath, the shape of her breasts rose. Morgan quickly stopped staring at the lovely petal soft glow of her bosom and looked instead at her dark eyes with their long curving lashes.

"Essie says your name is Morgan."

"Lee Morgan, at your service, madam." Saying his name began to make him feel more like himself. "And yours?"

"Celia Fair."

"Your name suits you." He hadn't meant to say it aloud. How fair she was, with her pale clear skin and auburn hair.

"*Miss* Celia Fair," she said.

Morgan was glad to hear that. He had not been above helping himself to some other man's woman in times past, always providing the woman was willing. But this one! He was somehow glad to hear it was Miss.

"But thanking you isn't all I came here for." Her eyes shot arrows into Morgan's heart and other vital places. "I came to ask another favor."

"Ask, by all means. Do you want to sit?" He removed his gunbelt from the chair and hung it on the bedpost.

"No. Thank you." Celia Fair shook her auburn curls. "I wanted to ask you to keep this for me." She held out the leather bag.

Morgan noticed again the carving in the leather, hand-tooling that could only have been done with loving care by an expert. "Did someone you know do that leather work?" he asked.

"My brother. A long time ago." There was a tone to the answer that said 'don't ask anything more about it.' She went on to explain the favor. "It would be only for a few days. If you could hold onto the bag, keep it safe for me, until the next stage comes through."

He accepted the bag. It was heavy. He thought he should not have left her standing there holding such a heavy burden.

"The next stage? You're not going away?"

She smiled up at him, warming him all over. "Not right now."

Morgan set the bag on the chair. "I'll find a safe place for it. It must be important to you."

"It is." She did not tell him what it contained.

He glanced around the room thinking where it might be best concealed, while he was out gold hunting with Broom. He would keep it safe for Celia Fair. He walked to the fireplace wall and started checking bricks. Around the corner beneath the mantel, he found a slightly loose one.

After working at it for a few moments with a knife he took from his right boot, he removed the brick and the one below it. There was a hollow space behind them. He took out four more bricks to make enough room for the bag to slip in. The bag fit as if the space was made for it. He pushed it back hard, and replaced the bricks so they looked as if they had not been moved.

Celia Fair stood close by watching every move. Morgan swept up the mortar dust he had dislodged and pinching bits of it up between his fingers, spit on it and then worked it around the brick.

He returned to the fireplace and picked up the hearth rug. He drew it across the spot on the floor until all trace of the dust was hidden away under the rug.

"Aren't you clever!" Celia exclaimed. She stepped to the corner of the fireplace and looked at the place where Morgan had replaced the brick. She dusted a tiny spot with her finger. "If no one actually put hands on it, they would never know."

His job done, Lee returned his attention to Celia.

She stood there before him, looking up at him, charging the room with her beauty and her scent. They stood close together, only inches separating them.

She raised her hand and touched his cheek. "You were hurt in the fight."

"Not much. Just a scratch." The cheek was warmer where her fingers made contact. He could imagine the split skin healing at her touch.

They gazed into each other's eyes. He took one of her hands in both of his. "You are lovely. I feel as if I had known you always."

Her answer surprised him, thrilled him. "I have known you always, too." She hesitated only a moment, then said, "And I want you, Lee Morgan."

He took her face in both his hands and kissed her ever so gently. She responded and the kiss became demanding. His arms encircled her and hers reached up to him.

In moments his lips went from her lips to her eyelids, to her ear lobes, to her slim elegant neck. Her breath came more quickly, she arched her body to his, and he kissed the mounts of the white breasts above her velvet bodice.

She drew away from him and he experienced a momentary panic, thinking she was going to leave. Instead she led him to the bed, pushed him gently into a sitting position and knelt before him.

"You saved me from that beast, the least I can do is make you more comfortable." She reached behind the heel of one of his boots and using her other hand on top of his foot, pulled the boots off, first one then the other. She peeled off his socks.

Thank God for the bath and the clean clothes, Lee thought.

When she had freed his feet, she stroked them with her dainty hands, sending lightning bolts clear up to his throat.

In a moment, she rose, sat beside him and took off her own black shoes. Reaching underneath her skirt, she unfastened things and slipped off one silk stocking. She must be a city lady. He wondered how long she had been in this town and how she got mixed up with Brant Corson. But she was here now.

Celia removed the other silk stocking and dropped it on the floor beside the first.

Morgan's heart pounded so loud he thought she would hear.

In a moment she stood again and faced him. He regained his feet and again put his lips down to hers. Her arms went up around his neck and their kiss clung from sweet, through insistent, to passionate. Again he tasted her ear lobes and kissed his way down her neck and found the crevice between her breasts. Her scent was light yet overpowering.

Finding the ends of the silver lacing, Lee pulled and loosened the velvet bodice that kept him from those tempting globes. As the nipples came into his view, they sprang to attention, the tips hardening before his lips reached them.

Celia's fingers combed through the hair at the back of his head, and drew him closer, then traced around his ears down his neck to unbutton his shirt. He let go of her long enough to snatch his shirt off and in moments they both were naked and again reaching out, each pulling the other close.

Morgan held the whole silkiness of her against himself, feeling every smooth soft inch of her on his body, once again kissing her lips. He felt the rapid beat of her heart against his chest, the rise of her breasts with their hard nipples. He kissed them again and tasted them with his tongue and lips, making gentle sucking motions.

He ran his hands over her smooth back, past her slim waist, and over the slight flare of her hips, feeling her shudder with pleasure at his touch.

Grasping her firm round buttocks, he pulled her tightly against him as he felt the rising pressure in his groin. He kissed his way down to her navel and circled it with his tongue, feeling goose bumps rise on her legs as he bent and let his hands traverse the rest of the way clear to her ankles.

He rose again and sought her lips. Celia's hands felt both soothing and exciting as they traced his contours, down his back—slowly, teasingly, caressingly—then circling his buttocks and up his sides and to his chest. His nipples contracted at her touch, as hers had to his.

Lee went down to one knee on the carpet and when his kisses reached the red-gold furry mound hiding the love place he sought, Celia's legs trembled. In a moment he stood and in the same motion lifted her in his arms and deposited her on the bed. He took a moment to gaze at the loveliness of the feast before him. Her eyes sparkled with eagerness.

He began at her breasts again and his kissing, gentle biting, and sucking made her squirm with pleasure and raise her lower body to invite him. His own organ urged him too, but he took his time.

Making his way again to the love nest, he parted its outer lips and let his tongue make dartings and sippings, over and over again. She was becoming damp with readiness, but he had flavors to taste before the main course.

He licked and tickled and sipped until she thrust herself harder into his face. He leaned in to her and thrust his tongue as far inside her as it would go, savoring the essence of her.

She yearned for more, for the real thing, and her fingers found his jewels and gently touched and fondled, then encircled his rod and coaxed it into even more hardness and length, until he understood her desire was as great as his own.

He was going to give her what she wanted, push it into her, because he was becoming eager too. But as he straightened above her, she deftly turned her body head to foot, so that while he could continue his tasting, she put her lips to his groin, kissing all around the base of his organ, fondling his balls with one hand, stroking and kissing up and down the length of his turgid penis with her tongue and lips.

Her tongue drew a path up the back of his rod, the most sensitive side. When she reached the tip, the end of her tongue circled it. Her touch was light at first, then became more firm and urgent.

Again Lee sent his tongue into her love hole. She shuddered and momentarily seemed to forget what she was about. She moaned as her opening made an involuntary grab at his tongue. Then she put her mouth over the end of him and nibbled with her lips, like a mare taking a sugar cube from a man's hand. The exquisite torment of holding back was almost too much for Lee, but before he could make a move, she twisted around again.

She pushed gently so that he lay on his back. She mounted him, holding his organ in her delicate hand as she lowered herself onto it, sighing with pleasure as she sat all the way down on him.

Then she rode.

She rode him like a delighted child galloping across a pasture. He put his hands up to clasp her bouncing breasts. He pressed his buttocks upward until her knees no longer touched the bed as she rode. She balanced herself with her hands on his chest and clamped her knees to his sides.

Her tempo fit his and he urged her to continue with his hands at her buttocks.

She romped merrily, smiling, throwing her head back and giving little laughs and joyful cries.

Then suddenly the world exploded in ecstasy. His whole being seemed to burst out into her. He thought he would never finish before he died of the exquisite release. Celia cried out with joy.

They pushed together hard, desperate to hold the moment, until finally she collapsed forward onto him. He put his arms around her to hold her close on top of him feeling a glorious pulsing, hearts pounding, and the sighing breaths of fulfillment.

After a while, they rolled over, nestled their bodies close together and sighed audibly again. They kissed softly and fell asleep.

When Morgan came awake in the morning, light pushed through the lace curtains showing through his eyelids into his soul. When had he slept so? Deep delicious rest.

He stretched, remembered, and reached out feeling for her across the bed.

Celia Fair was gone.

He lay there for a long moment wishing and wondering. But he knew women were like that. Here one moment in all their glory, and then gone. He had thought from time to time of settling down. Once in a while a woman came along that made settling down seem desirable. Celia Fair could have turned out to be one of those.

Morgan shook himself out of his reverie. The fair Celia was not here now. He had other things to do.

Morgan had to meet Broom to go out and see what the old man could tell them about the gold. He dressed, strapped on and tied down his Bisley Colts, and left the hotel.

The sun oozed over the eastern horizon making a long shadow of Lee Morgan's tall frame as he covered the fifty yards of the dusty main street of Lost Canyon. He mounted the three steps to the sand-whipped front door of the General Emporium.

Denims, stacked on a log table, filled one corner of the store, and sheepskin jackets for sale hung on nails pounded into the wall. Dried beans in an open sack leaned against the tin covered counter where an aproned clerk weighed sugar on a scoop scale.

Morgan needed a rifle. He ran his fingers along the barrel of a .52 caliber Spencer, checked the sighting twice and nodded. He laid three tubes of ammunition beside it and paid. A pretty girl entered the store. Morgan smiled and tipped his tan Stetson.

Morgan picked up his purchases and was ready to leave as Hank Broom stepped briskly into the Emporium. "Thought I'd find you here."

For most of his forty years, Broom had lived by his gun, and sent a few men, good and bad to their maker. He was still quick as a fox. Sometimes too quick for his own good, Morgan thought.

The two stopped at the cafe for coffee, eggs, steak and hash browns. They said little as they ate, intent only on getting set for their morning errand. As they got up from the table, Morgan slipped a couple lumps of sugar into his pocket.

"I've got it," Broom said and paid for the meal.

It was Broom's show, so Morgan didn't argue.

Outside, an eddy of dust swirled and Broom pulled his hat forward to shield his face. They turned toward the livery. "There's a fair looking bay for sale, stabled beside my mount, a gelding. Young, strong, don't know the price. Stable hand says a fellow sold it for a stake in a poker game. He lost."

"I'll take a look."

The gelding suited Morgan. He added a saddle and dickered the stable owner down to a suitable price. After paying the man, Morgan saddled his new horse and looped his black snake whip over the saddle horn, then stepped to the horse's head. He stroked the bay's muzzle. "We'll get along fine. Won't we, fella?" The horse poked his nose forward. Morgan reached into his pocket and brought out the sugar cubes. The bay accepted one, then the other. Morgan patted the horse's neck and mounted up.

He and Broom headed out of town.

"This old timer you think might know something about where the gold is hidden, he got a name?"

"Ole, but everybody calls him Gramps. For some reason, Hex Downs, the one who hid the gold bars, got friendly with Gramps. I was in town the day Hex arrived. Close mouthed. Wouldn't even give his name at first, then finally said he was Hex Downs."

Broom paused to motion a slight change in direction. "I had just come in from Sacramento. The papers up there were full of the train robbery. No names were mentioned, just that one got away. The story said which way they thought he headed." Broom grinned. "Not many newspapers come to Lost Canyon. Don't suppose most of the people can read anyhow."

Morgan gazed ahead at the cool green trees on the side of the mountain a few miles ahead. "How did you find the cabin?"

"Followed Downs up there. After Hex died in the gunfight, I went up and talked to the old fellow. He's smart and wary of strangers. I doubt anybody puts much over on him. He's a good man, and fair. I didn't get it out of him, but I think Downs told him where he hid the gold."

Broom took a long drink of water from his canteen and offered it to Morgan. The morning had begun to heat up.

An hour later the trail led the two men into the trees. Live oak leaves rustled in the breeze and covered much of the ground. Suddenly the trail all but disappeared. Now it skirted the oak, then turned north back into the high desert.

When they reached the pines, only hoof tracks showed them the way. "Gramps have horses?" Morgan asked.

Broom squinted at the tracks. "The Indians do a little hunting up here, jackrabbits that wander up from the desert, now and then wild turkey. The old Chief is peacable enough, tolerates the white man. But he's got a son who hates us. Wants the Washos to be fighting warriors, as they have in the past."

This was new country to Morgan, and he listened for foreign sounds. Nothing stirred that he could detect.

They were most of a mile into the timber when an arrow skimmed Broom's shoulder and lodged in a Ponderosa Pine. Birds flew up in a flurry of movement. Both men hit the ground at the same time.

Quiet. Deep dead quiet.

"Damn," Morgan muttered. "You can't hear them and you can't see them."

Crouched low, they led their horses into the trees and took shelter behind two downed trees. Both leveled their rifles in the direction the arrow had come from and waited.

Morgan knew they were being surrounded. He could feel it by the cold chill that crossed his neck. He rolled toward Broom. "See anything?"

Broom pointed first in one direction, then in another. "Could be half a dozen of them, probably after our guns and horses."

"Washos?"

Broom nodded.

A dry leaf crunched. Morgan fired. Two arrows skimmed the top of the log where Morgan crouched. He went lower just in time.

"Cover me." Morgan plunged into a stand of pine a few yards away skidding on his stomach the last few feet. Two more arrows twanged into the ground where he'd first hit the dirt.

He crouched, eyes boring through the trees. A gust of wind rippled through, making false sounds. He held his fire. He could hear Broom's rifle shots zinging over his head.

A horse whinnied. Morgan turned. Broom's .45 pistol exploded. An Indian yelled, then dropped a few feet from the horses. Three arrows returned fire. One pinned Broom's shirt sleeve to one of the downed logs. His shirt ripped when he jerked loose. Blood showed on his shirt; he was hit.

Morgan made a slow careful circle attempting to get behind the Indians. There had to be at least three left. How many more? Thick brush blocked his view. Slowly he got to his feet behind a tall pine.

He scanned the thick stand of trees. He listened for some telltale sound. The bastards could be anywhere, and Broom couldn't make a dash for the protection of the thicker stand of trees without cover.

Morgan backed stealthily toward another tree. He sensed a presence. He whipped his Bisley from his holster and turned just as a brown arm reached for his neck. He could smell the Indian's sweat. A knife, aimed at his chest, glistened in a shaft of sunlight.

Morgan fired. The Indian dropped without a sound, a hole where his nose had been. The knife slipped from his fingers. Morgan kicked it away.

Morgan picked up his hat and set it back on his head. For the next half hour he crept through the trees. Because of the arrows shot at Broom, there had to be at least two more. He thought about returning to where Broom still lay between the two downed trees, but until he got those last two bastards they couldn't go on to the cabin anyhow.

A bird sound close by warned him, because it wasn't a bird call, it was a signal. Morgan pushed his rear into some thick brush and backed in until he was out of sight, but he wasn't fast enough. An Indian, his face contorted with rage, plunged at him with a war ax raised to strike. Morgan lifted his Bisley and fired. The Indian stopped mid-plunge, a bullet between his eyes. He dropped to the ground.

Morgan let the air swish out of his lungs. Damn, he hated fighting Indians. They were sneaky and so silent.

He glanced toward Broom's spot between the downed trees. He was gone. How in hell had he gotten out of the tight spot he was in? A shot from a forty-five sounded, then another. Morgan waited.

In a moment, Broom emerged from the trees; the spot of blood on his torn shirt sleeve had not widened. He hoisted his rifle over his shoulder and called out to Morgan. "Must be slippin'. I didn't get him. But he was moving out fast. I think that's the last of them."

The two men made their way back to the horses.

"The Washos want guns, and now and then they get a few." Broom shoved his rifle into the saddle boot. "But they didn't get ours."

Morgan motioned toward a rise. "We better make sure that last one was headed for home. I don't want any arrows in my back."

Broom agreed.

For several minutes the two men, astride their mounts, watched the valley below. A galloping horse, carrying one Indian, with three riderless horses tethered behind, grew rapidly smaller going away along the lower trail.

Morgan and Broom headed back to their path to the cabin.

"How's that arm?"

Broom reined in and waited for Lee. "Just a nick, I'll clean it up when we get to the cabin. I got a glimpse of that Indian that got away. I think it was the old Chief's son."

"Did he see you?"

Broom nodded. "And if he's anything like I've heard, he'll be after me. I'd better keep my rear covered."

"Don't you usually?"

The trail widened and Broom and Morgan rode side by side.

"Tell me something about this Hex Downs," Morgan said. "I gather he was a good shot, but he went down in a shootout?"

"He was shot in the back. Nobody, including the sheriff seemed to figure out who or why."

"Why did he come to Lost Canyon in the first place, and what made him stay?"

"He was here only a month or so." Broom frowned thoughtfully. "I didn't get well acquainted with the man. Don't think anybody did really. But I watched him. I would say he came to Lost Canyon by accident. The train was robbed this side of Sacramento. His partner

was killed in the robbery and Downs ran."
Broom shrugged. "It's only a guess, but I think
he figured there were a lot of lawmen in
Sacramento, and he'd be safer to go east."

"There's nothing east of Lost Canyon but
desert."

"That's right. Once he hit this settlement, he
didn't dare head on down into the desert alone
in the middle of summer. It not only skirts the
Washo Indian camp, but he couldn't carry
enough water to get him through. Not with
forty pounds of gold in his saddle bags."

"Did he make friends with anybody in town?"

"No. He sat around in the bar with Corson,
the fellow you horsewhipped." Broom grinned.
"I think Corson was trying to get close to him.
But I don't think they were friends, least not
friendly enough so Downs would tell Corson
where the gold was hidden. Once he met
Gramps in town, Hex spent a lot of time up
here."

Morgan could understand why. The altitude
and the pine trees changed the summer heat of
Lost Canyon, which was a couple of thousand
feet lower elevation, to a cooler mountain
temperature. He glanced at the wide flat valley
below. Heat rose in waves from some areas far
beyond them and to the east.

They stopped to rest the horses from the
steep climb of the last few miles.

"This Hex Downs could have been anybody,"
Morgan said. "Maybe he was passing through
and liked the town. Decided to stay."

"You know me better than that. I don't chase
wild hares." Broom frowned at Morgan. "Hex
Downs was the man with the gold, all right.

Now all we need is to find out what he did with it."

They resumed their ride and an hour passed before the cabin came into sight. It was a one room hutch, maybe twelve-by-fifteen feet, neatly built of logs. A lean-to held fire wood, and a tethered mule brayed as they approached.

The cabin door stood open.

Morgan didn't like the wary feeling that assailed him. From habit his right hand slid to his tied down Bisley Colts. Fresh hoof prints from shod horses stood out in the dirt to the left of the door.

Broom dismounted, rifle in hand. So Broom felt it, too.

Silently they approached the open door, one on each side. Broom stepped boldly forward. Morgan held up a hand, then shook his head. Broom stopped. They both listened for any tell-tale sound that could designate danger inside.

Silence.

Could the old man have heard the shots earlier from this distance and expected trouble? From what Broom had told him about Gramps, Morgan didn't think he was the kind of man to shoot before he knew who he was shooting at.

"Gramps?" Broom called out.

No answer.

Broom lowered his rifle. "He's not even here. Probably down at the spring."

They edged their way into the cabin, Morgan still held his Bisley Colts ready to use.

"Damn!" Broom exploded. "Look at this mess."

They stood inside for a long moment to

accustom their eyes to the gloom. Chairs were
overturned, boxes dumped on the floor, and the
plank table lay on its side.

On the bunk in the far corner of the room lay
Gramps. Blood covered one side of his face. His
eyes stared at them in death.

Morgan felt for a pulse even though he knew
the old timer was dead. The body was still
warm. Morgan closed the man's eyes.

"Looks like you weren't the only one, Hank,
who figured Gramps knew where the gold was
hidden."

3

Lee Morgan set a log chair on its feet and straddled it, leaning his forearms on the back. He ran a finger along the smoothly crafted chair back, feeling the workmanship. "Whatever Gramp's killer was looking for, he didn't find it."

"That figures. They probably killed the old man tryin' to make him talk, then tore the place up looking for the gold or something that would lead them to it." Broom picked up four books that had been dumped to the floor and set them back on the shelf. "It's obvious the old fellow could read, maybe he could write too and wrote something down about the gold."

"I think he was too smart for that." Morgan's gaze took in the empty shelves and the spattered floor. Sticky preserves ran together with tomatoes and cut green beans. "Every jar has been broken and searched and every box has been dumped." He indicated the pile of clothes with turned out pockets. "They even went through his clothes. No, I'd guess they found nothing. But that doesn't mean we can't find something that might tell us who did the killing. At least we know one thing for sure."

"What's that?"

"Somebody else knows that Hex Downs brought gold bars to Lost Canyon."

"When we find out who killed Gramps, we'll know."

Lee gently spread a blanket over the old man's body. "Wonder who the old fellow was protecting by keeping silent. Downs is dead, and somehow I can't believe the old gent wanted the gold for himself, or he'd have already had it and gone off to spend it."

"Gold is a mighty powerful magnet." Broom began a close search of the far side of the cabin. He added to his philosophy on gold, "Some people, even honest folks, can't resist the pull."

Morgan gave a muffled chuckle. "Even honest folks like you and me."

Morgan combed the side of the room where Gramps lay dead on his bunk. It was beginning to look like their prime lead would get them nowhere. He ran his fingers along all edges of the bunk, hoping for a secret compartment, or a niche, anything the killers had missed.

Morgan's fingers stopped. "Broom, I may have found something." Down on one knee, he examined a scrap of leather wedged between the two birch logs that formed one side of the bunk.

Broom leaned down to look, his salt and pepper hair fell across his forehead. "Could be." He lessened the tension of the logs and Morgan pulled the piece of buckskin free. They examined the three inch strip, about a quarter of an inch wide, turned it over.

Morgan ran it between his fingers. "Feel this, it's soft, too soft for home tanning, I'd say. I've got an old buckskin jacket back in Idaho."

Broom nodded in agreement. "Didn't see any

clothes here with that sort of trim." He paused a moment, then said. "Well, hell, guess we'd better get the sheriff notified, so we can bury the old fellow."

Morgan slipped the scrap of leather into his pocket, dusted off his Stetson, from habit, and set it firmly on his head. "Coming?" He opened the cabin door and took one step. A volley of gunfire pushed him back fast. "Damn! Now somebody else wants us dead."

Morgan's Bisley Colts jumped into his hand and he returned four shots into a clump of trees a hundred feet away. He glanced at Broom sighting his rifle through the small window. "Think it's the Indian back with reinforcements?"

"If they had revolvers they would have used them the first time." He pointed toward a neat circle of shots, head high, that the gunman had made in the cabin door. "That's good shooting for close to a hundred feet. That was no Indian."

"I'm going out the back window and try to get behind them. We haven't got enough ammunition to last an hour in here. Keep 'em occupied." Morgan dumped the spent shells from the Bisley Colts, loaded in six new rounds and dropped a handful of shells into a pocket. He picked up his black snake whip and disappeared over the sill of the back window.

Morgan heard Broom's two well-placed rifle shots plow into the clump of trees. A dozen, maybe more, shots answered, hitting the cabin above and below Broom's window. Then more shots from the trees, even when Broom didn't shoot back.

Morgan circled behind the clump of trees,

giving it a wide berth. Inch by silent inch he crept toward the sound of the gunfire. He could smell the gunpowder, even taste it on his tongue. Whoever was doing the shooting, meant business.

He crept closer. He'd have to take them one at a time.

Behind an enormous rock, a battered brown felt hat bobbed first one way and then the other, avoiding splinters from the rocks that Broom targeted with his rifle.

Morgan listened for firing from some other location. There was none. For one gunny, he sure raised a ruckus.

Morgan crept closer behind the pistol-packing assailant. He wasn't in the habit of shooting men in the back, not even killers.

Morgan raised the black snake whip. He wanted this one alive. If he knew anything about the gold, Morgan planned to squeeze it out of him.

The tip of the black snake circled the gun, whipping it to the ground. Without missing a beat, the man spun around, his other gun firing at where Morgan's head would have been had he not dropped to the ground and rolled.

Morgan came up squeezing the trigger of his Bisley. The other man's gun clicked, clicked again. Empty. He could not fire again without reloading.

A breeze lifted the other man's hat. It floated to the ground. He shook aside a shock of sun-bleached hair.

Morgan's trigger finger froze. "My God, you're nothing but a damn kid."

"I'm not a kid. I'm eighteen, and I'll get you if I have to . . . to . . ."

Morgan came closer. The kid didn't back away. He had guts all right. The kid had guts. His Bisley Colts still aimed at the kid's chest, he took the useless pistol from the boy's hand and tossed it into the brush. The gun on the ground, he kicked it out of reach. "You'll get me if you have to what?" Morgan snapped.

The boy stood straight and tall. He wore bib overalls over a blue-gray cotton shirt. Morgan would bet a night's stake in a poker game the kid had never even shaved.

The boy's eyes blazed with fury. "If I have to hang for it. Gramps was my friend. You killed him."

"Or you did."

"Me! Gramps was all I had in this rotten world. He raised me up from a little kid. Taught me everything I know."

"Sit down," Morgan ordered, and pointed to a patch of grass in the shade. Warily the boy sat down, not taking his eyes from Morgan for a second. Morgan dropped down beside him. "You got a name?"

"Jason. Jason Isley."

"Jason," Morgan said. "I didn't beat your Gramps to death, and neither did Hank Broom, my partner. How did you know he was dead? He was still warm when we got here."

"I found him." Jason's eyes clouded with grief. "I heard somebody coming, and I jumped through the back window and ran. I thought it was the killers coming back."

"Didn't you see anybody going down the mountain? You must have seen something. Whoever did this had to go down." Morgan looked beyond the cabin. Only a small rocky rise showed the top of the mountain. "There's no place to go up to. Broom says it's a sheer drop on the other side."

"There's a trail that goes all the way down to the high desert, but it's hard to find. Somebody would have to know his way around."

"And who might that be?"

Jason frowned impatiently. "How would I know? I never use it."

"Seems to me you don't know much of anything except how to shoot a gun at anybody you see."

"I heard you and your friend coming."

"What about the Indian fight. You hear that?"

Jason nodded. "I saw Burning Arrow scoot for camp with three horses behind him. Did he leave any dead Indians behind?"

"Three."

"That's right. There could be trouble. But I suppose as long as his son didn't get hurt, the old chief won't start anything. He's old and he wants peace with the whites. It's Burning Arrow and a bunch of young braves who think the tribe should still be warriors."

"So Broom told me."

Jason glanced at Morgan. "Gramps and the old chief are . . . were, friends."

Morgan got to his feet and motioned to the cabin with his head. "Come on, we'll tell Broom who you are, then you go down and get the sheriff. Broom's been around here longer than I have, and he says to be on the safe side, we can't bury your Gramps until the sheriff checks it out."

"I heard Sheriff Taylor telling somebody that you're a dangerous gunny and that you and Broom used to be partners holding up banks.

Did the ranchers outside of town hire you?"

"Hank Broom and I were never partners in
any such thing, just friends from a long time
ago. Why would the ranchers hire me. Have
they got rustler trouble?"

Jason seemed relieved. "I should have known
the sheriff wasn't telling the truth, he lies to
everybody."

"Even to the ranchers?"

"He doesn't even try to catch the rustlers."

Morgan let Jason get his pistols out of the
brush. "Can't let 'em lie out here and rust."
Then they headed for the cabin.

Morgan pushed open the cabin door. Broom
sat across the room, his rifle leveled. He let it
fall to his knee. "Hello, Isley. Where are the
others, dead?"

Morgan grinned. "Wasn't anybody else. This
one-man army did all the shooting."

"Waste of ammunition," Broom said. "What
did you plan to do when you ran out?"

"I separated you two, didn't I? Made one of
you go out the window. Once I got you, I
planned to go after the other one."

Broom shook his head. "You'd need eyes at
the back of your head to watch both of us."

"Okay, cut the lesson in strategy," Morgan
growled. "Jason, who knew Hex Downs spent a
lot of time up here, besides you?"

"I don't live up here now. I live in a room
behind the cafe downtown, I work there. I never
saw Downs here. But Gramps said Hex came up
now and then."

"This is a long hot ride from town. Did he tell
you why Hex came up here?"

Jason glanced warily from Broom to Morgan.
"Does there have to be a reason?" He slapped

his worn felt hat on his head and loaded his pistols. "I'll get the sheriff. I'd like to bury Gramps before nightfall."

"Take my horse," Morgan said.

"No. Mine's over behind the rocks."

Jason walked a good piece into the timber before he permitted a quiet tear to slide down his cheek. Gramps was dead. It was like he'd lost a mother and father at the same time. He walked faster hoping the awful ache would go away.

In the distance, Jason's horse, Felipe, whinnied. He was up wind from the horse and Jason wondered absently how the animal could know he was coming.

With no sense of caution, Jason called out. "I'm coming, Felipe, keep your shirt on."

Jason rounded the boulder that shielded the horse from view. All thoughts of Gramps vanished. The smell of danger permeated the air. He dropped to the ground a half second before a rifle shot cracked against the rock behind him.

Jason had flipped a rein around a flat ground rock to keep Felipe out of sight after he had discovered Gramps' body.

It was a good place to hide a horse. Two thirty-foot boulders formed a wide V. At the narrow part, they almost came together, leaving a six foot deep hiding place. When he was a kid he used to hide from Gramps when it was time to do his reading and numbers.

Now Jason crawled along the sandy ground, using his horse as a shield. The rifle shot had come from a stand of trees fifty yards away. A bullet skidded across the ground. Felipe whinnied and pulled back as far as the anchored rein would permit.

Jason reached for the flat rock. Another shot skipped across the hard dirt landing useless against the rocky wall.

He had to get Felipe loose so he could get away. Gramps had given him Felipe on his birthday the year he was twelve. He couldn't bear to lose Felipe now.

Crawling forward, Jason jerked the rein loose, then plunged for the small hiding place and protection. The horse raced for freedom. He would go home to the stable in Lost Canyon, or maybe just back to the cabin.

A barrage of gunfire erupted from the trees. Jason unloaded both his pistols at the clump of greenery, then backed into the narrow rock opening to reload. Morgan had called him a one-man army. Jason hoped the man with the rifle would think he had more than one man to shoot down.

He backed deeper into the narrow space. The gunman took advantage of the seconds Jason was silent. Three rifle shots in quick succession hit the inner edge of his hiding place.

Jason stepped back. All hell broke loose. Bullets flew in every direction ricocheting from one side of his hiding place to the other. Jason dived out the other side to keep from getting killed.

When the barrage of stray bullets finally stopped, Jason aimed both guns at the trees. He squinted into the noonday sun.

For just a second a face emerged from the trees. Corson. Why was Corson trying to kill him? Jason didn't fire.

He heard horses coming then. They came from the direction of the cabin. Probably

Morgan and Broom. They had likely heard the shooting.

Movement in the trees brought Jason's attention back to Corson, then an ominous quiet. Had Corson heard the approach of horses, too? Cautiously Jason moved from his hiding place. No firing came from the trees.

He stepped onto the trail. Morgan and Broom reined in their mounts, settling them down from the sudden stop. Morgan looked down at Jason and shook his head. "Can't you get even a mile on your way without getting shot at? Did you get him?"

"No." Jason spat indignantly. "But if you hadn't come pounding down the trail, I would have. It was Brant Corson. He ran. I saw him."

"Horse came up to the cabin with no rider. We didn't figure you preferred to walk to town." Morgan's forehead wrinkled thoughtfully. "So Corson tried to kill you. He also tried to do something to Celia Fair. Looks as though he's the man we have to get. He must know about the gold. When he couldn't get information from the old timer back there, no doubt he intends to get rid of anybody else who knows."

Broom nodded. "Corson. Turd. He'd kill his own mother for a double eagle. Wonder who he's working with, or if he's goin' it alone."

"Do you think he killed Gramps?" Jason asked.

"When we got to the cabin," Broom answered, "there were footprints in the dirt, looked like two horses."

Morgan dismounted and handed Jason the reins. "Take my horse back up to get yours. Be careful, Corson could be waiting for you to start down the hill. He's out to get you, and he might not be the only one. Don't trust anybody in town, and I mean nobody until we get this sorted out. Now go get the sheriff and stick close to him all the way back up here. At least with him you should be safe."

Back at the cabin, Morgan motioned to Broom to sit on the step. For several minutes the two of them sat quietly soaking up the beauty of the trees, the cool shade, and the cloudless sky where it showed through. Broom rolled a cigarette and lit it, making sure his match was out instead of just throwing it in the brush. It had been a dry year so far. A few feet away, Broom's horse stood beside Morgan's, munching the crisp green grass.

"The old fellow owned what must be the only decent patch of green in the area," Morgan said. "Must be twenty degrees cooler up here than it is down in the middle of that burning town." He turned abruptly. "Do you think the gold is up here? We'd better keep looking before Jason gets back with the sheriff."

Broom stood up. "No, I don't think it's here, but if we get off our butts and really look, we may find another lead. When I telegraphed you to come, Gramps was the only lead I had. That and some talk around town."

Morgan grinned and got to his feet. "I didn't exactly plan on fighting Indians or getting into a race with half a town to locate a few gold bars."

"Nothing comes easy, Morgan, you should know that by now." Broom winked. "Not even that Celia Fair. You seem to be having a hell of a time keeping up with her."

For the next several hours, they searched for some clue that would lead them to the gold. Outside, Broom dug at the base of every tree

with fresh dirt marks around it. When nothing
led anywhere they began all over again in the
one-room cabin.

"Books," Morgan said. "The old fellow
seemed to set a lot of store by books." One at a
time he leafed through them. Through Dickens,
and a History of Sweden. Ole Olmanson was
written in the fly leaf of some of the books.
Must have been the old man's whole name. A
Swede. There was a worn Bible, with names and
dates written. All the dates were too old to
mean anything.

A beginning reader. Morgan smiled. He'd
learned some from the same reader when he went
to school.

Next he picked up a threadbare dictionary. He
fanned the pages. A thin oilskin folder dropped
to the floor. He opened it and found a leaf of
yellowed papers. "Hey, Broom, look at this."
Morgan read aloud. "Being of sound mind I
bequeath all my earthly possessions to Jason
Isley." There was more legal jargon, describing
the cabin and the land surrounding it and any
and all livestock. "It's witnessed by Jeb and
Essie Rowe. They're the ones who own the
hotel?"

"That's them." Broom reread the paper. "It's
even been made up by a legal man. He's dead
now. Used to be a judge."

"At least the kid will have something besides
washing dishes and the like in the cafe."
Morgan looked out the door. "Here he comes
now with the sheriff. Should we give the will to
the sheriff so he can finish making it legal?"

"No!" Broom exploded. "Give it to Jason,
later. Let him decide who he wants to show it to.
Probably should take it up to Sacramento and

have it recorded right and proper. That way nobody's gonna cheat him out of it."

Morgan quickly folded the papers back into the oilskin and shoved it into his back pocket.

It was nearly four o'clock by Morgan's pocket Waterbury, when Jason and the sheriff reined in their horses and came inside the cabin.

The sheriff jerked back the blanket that covered the old man, then dropped it back into place. "That's him. Beaten to death, huh?" The sheriff dropped his ample body into the one easy chair in the room and pushed his expensive gray Stetson to the back of his head. A shock of black hair fell across his brow making his oily face appear swarthy. "Anybody see who did it?"

Jason looked away. "He was dead when I found him, Sheriff."

"I can see that." He shot an accusing glance at Morgan. "You're a professional gunny. Did you try to beat information out of the old codger?"

Morgan didn't bother to answer, but Broom did. "Morgan is a friend of mine, and he did not beat Gramps to death. We found him together, and he was dead."

"Good thing you got Broom here to vouch for you, Morgan, though he ain't much better. Otherwise, I'd lock you up in a minute. Strangers, that's what causes trouble around Lost Canyon. Strangers poking their noses into things that are none of their business."

He got up and walked to the door. "Go ahead and plant him."

Jason jumped to his feet. "Aren't you going to try to find out who killed Gramps? You haven't even looked around the cabin, for footprints or something."

"All in good time, boy. I figure it must have been a stranger coming through who counted on the old man having a few double eagles tucked away. Probably never see him again, unless he comes back."

"Brant Corson isn't a stranger in town, but he was out back shooting at young Isley," Morgan said. "Just after noon time, before the kid left for town to get you."

"You're just trying to get Corson into trouble because you had a run-in with him," the sheriff said.

Neither Broom nor Jason Isley argued with him.

The sheriff pointed a threatening forefinger at Morgan. "You, Morgan, I want out of town. We don't want the likes of you shooting up our town and riling up the Indians. You better not be here tomorrow."

When the sheriff had gone, Broom and Morgan helped dig the grave. They wrapped Ole Olmanson in a blanket and lowered him into the earth.

They stood for a moment before shoveling the dirt back over him, Jason a little apart from the other two.

Morgan mumbled to Broom in a low voice. "Suppose we should say something?"

"I guess so. You want to?"

"You. You're the preacher's son."

Broom accordingly bowed his head and asked the Lord's blessing on the old man's soul. He used his name, Ole Olmanson, and then said, "Known and liked by all as Gramps. Amen."

Jason said, "Thank you."

They took up their shovels and filled in the

grave, smoothing it up around the sides. Then Morgan and Broom returned the tools to the shed, leaving Jason alone.

4

Jason Isley felt empty. He stood alone under the
trees beside the mound of newly turned earth.
All the rest of the world was out there and he
was here, alone.

The brief informal ceremony was over, the
poor old man's body was in the ground. It had
been kind of Lee Morgan, he thought, to suggest
that they should say a few words for the old
man. Jason guessed he wouldn't have thought
of it himself. Or perhaps he would have when it
was too late.

Gramps had been the only person Jason could
remember who had seemed like family. Other
boys had a mother and a father, sometimes
brothers and sisters. But Jason had only
Gramps.

The man, who Jason was later told had been
his father, had never made a home for his wife
and child. He rode away one day when Jason
had not yet reached the age of two, and was
later hanged as a cattle thief. As Jason reached
the age of reason, he learned about his father.
Since that time he grew up wanting nothing to
do with law-breakers of any kind.

Old Gramps had been able to see the good in
most anyone, but Jason saw right and wrong.

He barely remembered his mother. He had a picture of her tucked in with his meager belongings. She had been a pretty lady. Maybe not a very good lady, but a pretty lady. She had died giving birth to another baby, who also had a hit and run father, just as Jason did. But that baby died with their mother.

Jason was about four years old when she died, and Gramps had taken him in. He could not remember any home but here in the cabin with Gramps.

Gramps taught Jason to ride before he was big enough to get on the horse alone. He had taught him other things, too. He read to Jason from books and magazines and newspapers that came from big cities back east.

When Jason was about six, Gramps had given him a horse, and had insisted that Jason ride the horse to the one-room school house on the edge of town where there was sometimes a schoolmarm or a school master. When there was no teacher and no school, or when the winter snows were too deep to get through, Gramps taught him.

Once Jason asked Gramps where he got his learning and Gramps just said, "Here and there. But that was a long time ago."

Jason was one of the few in town who had graduated the eighth grade and had taken all the tests. Gramps said that learning was an important thing.

When Jason turned sixteen, he had moved out of the cabin and got himself a proper job at the cafe in town so he could earn his own way. He came to see Gramps often and sometimes brought him supplies from town. If he had been living here still, maybe this wouldn't have happened. Maybe Gramps would still be alive. Or maybe they would both be dead.

Surely Jason would have been able to do something to prevent whoever it was from killing the poor old man.

After a little while, as the breeze pushed at the thatch of sun-bleached hair falling over his forehead, Jason took a deep breath and turned away from the grave. He walked a little way toward the cabin and then stooped to pick up a small round stone about the size of a silver dollar. He held it and looked at it, then found another and another.

He gathered a handful of the worn pellets, rounded by weather and boots tramping the path. Smoothing them in his hand one by one, he thought, Gramps had always appreciated things like this, smooth stones, weathered wood, the way a hawk soared across the sky from one great tree to a rock on the side of the mountain.

Jason returned to the mound and placed the stones in a circle at the head of the grave in front of the wooden cross that Hank Broom had set into the dirt.

"Jason." He heard Lee Morgan's voice call.

Without answering, Jason made his way back to the cabin.

"We were picking up some of this stuff before," Morgan told him. "You'll be interested in this paper here. Seems to be the old man's will."

"Gramps left a will?" Jason looked at the paper. The document was typewritten on a legal looking form. It had Gramps' signature: Ole Olmanson, and some other signers had put their names to it, one of them with curliques at the ends of the letters.

"And there's some other stuff here that tells the lawyer's name who drew up the will." Morgan handed the rest of the papers over. "Broom says he was a judge, but he's dead now. You probably should go to Sacramento and get it registered, or something. You ever been to Sacramento?"

"No. I've never been to a big city. Always thought I'd like to some day." Jason sighed. "I don't have money enough to go there. But I could write a letter to the circuit judge. He'd be able to tell me what to do." Jason's mind raced with what he had just read. He owned land. Gramps had left him the land, the cabin, even old Rocky, the mule, because it said, *any and all livestock*.

"I wonder when he did this?"

"It's dated, isn't it?" Hank wanted to know.

"Oh, yes. That was a long time ago." Jason had trouble taking it all in. "Did Gramps think he was going to die way back when I was a little kid?"

"Guess he just wanted to be prepared, in case." Morgan patted Jason's shoulder. "Guess he really thought a lot of you, kid."

Jason folded the papers and put them back into the oilskin in which Morgan had found them. "I wonder why they didn't take these. Whoever killed him, I mean. The land's worth something. Couldn't they have had it instead of me?"

Hank Broom snorted. "Wasn't what they were after. They wanted information. Don't guess they got it, or they wouldn't have tore the place apart like it was."

"Probably didn't look through the books."

Morgan added. "Or even if they saw them, they'd likely think the boy here knew about the papers and the lawyer."

Broom agreed. Then he told Morgan they had best get back into town. "You comin' along, kid?"

"No," Jason told them. "I'll feed the mule and decide what to do next. I'll be on in soon. Got to go to work early in the morning."

Morgan put out his hand. "Good meeting you, Jason Isley. Sorry about your Gramps."

The younger man shook hands. He liked Morgan. "Thanks. Sure had you pegged wrong when I saw you ride up. You've been a help. Gramps probably woulda liked you, too."

"Sure you don't want to ride on into town with us?" Morgan asked. "Besides the trouble we had with those renegade Indians, whoever killed the old man might be looking for you."

Jason had avoided telling Morgan and Broom anything he knew about the gold, which was practically nothing. He knew that's what they were looking for too, but they weren't going to kill for it. "I can't tell them anything," he said. "Gramps probably knew. But he never told me."

"They don't know that," Broom said.

More thinking aloud, than actually telling, Jason said, "Gramps could have told Miss Celia."

"Celia?" Morgan asked.

"Well, he knew her. He talked to her, I guess about her brother."

"What brother?" Morgan pressed for more information. "You mean Celia Fair?"

"I guess that's her name. I don't know anything about it." Jason felt he had already said too much. "What are you guys going to do with that gold if you find it? It was stolen, wasn't it? Whose is it supposed to be?"

"Maybe we'll get a reward," Broom said smoothly.

Jason didn't believe him. He was sure that Broom and Morgan would never do something like kill a defenseless old man, but he didn't think they would turn in the gold if they found it. "You guys go ahead," he told them. "I'll see you in town. I'll be okay. Don't worry about me."

Finally Broom went down to the spring, filled the canteen and watered the horses. Then the two men set out on the return trip to town. They kept a sharp lookout but saw no one else anywhere along the trail on the uneventful ride back.

"Think the kid knows more than he's telling?" Broom asked once on the way.

Morgan shook his head. "No. But somebody else could have the idea that he does. Maybe we can track down those somebodies before they do any more damage. Might start with Brant Corson."

They rode out of the timber and down to the high desert feeling the afternoon heat start their sweat glands pouring before they reached the valley town of Lost Canyon.

They made the usual necessary arrangements and stabled their horses at the livery. Broom asked the stableman whether any other mounts kept there belonged to men recently arrived in town. The man didn't have a lot to say, so they learned nothing.

"The sheriff already asked you about that?" Morgan wanted to know.

"Sheriff and me don't talk much."

Morgan gave it up and followed Broom outside.

As they stood by the door deciding what they wanted to do next, the young boy and his dog that they had seen the day before, came around the side of the building. This time the boy didn't just look as if he wanted to say something.

Staring at Morgan, he said, "Hey, Mister. You're the guy what whupped old Brant Corson, ain't you?"

Morgan shrugged. "You might say so."

"Wished I could do that." His gaze slid to the black snake whip Morgan carried with him when he left the horse and saddle.

Broom laughed. "Maybe you could teach the kid something, Lee."

Morgan shook his head. "Doubt I'll be around long enough to give out any lessons."

The boy's wideeyed admiration shifted again to Morgan's face. "Bet you could even whup Sheriff Tyler."

"Would you like that?" Broom asked him.

The stableman appeared in the doorway. "Willy, you shut your mouth."

Willy tucked his head. "Aw, Pa." The boy and his dog shot around the side of the livery stable out of sight.

Morgan and Broom walked over to the hotel.

"Don't seem to be a lot of people in love with the sheriff in this town," Broom said.

"Probably a lot of people in this town have good sense. Sheriff Tyler seems like real shit. You known him long?"

"Wasn't sheriff last time I was in town. Never met him before."

They went on into the hotel.

"Gotta figure out what's next, I guess," Broom said and followed Morgan up to his room.

Opening the door, Morgan stopped dead. "What the hell!"

The room had been ransacked. Whoever did it had not taken care to cover his actions. The bureau drawers had been flung onto the floor, along with Morgan's few clean clothes. The bed had been turned up, the mattress dragged to the floor, blankets yanked every which way. His carpetbag lay on top of the pile of bedclothes.

It was the same sort of mess they had encountered at the old man's cabin. Except that Morgan didn't have as much stuff in his hotel room, so whoever had done it didn't find as much to toss around.

"They must have been mighty disappointed that you were traveling so light," Broom said, shoving his hat back and scratching his head. "What'd they think you had? You didn't rob a train on the way out, did you?"

"Nope."

There was only one thing that Morgan could figure would have caused this. He had rescued Celia Fair, and Celia had come to him to leave something that she obviously treasured.

Broom was no dummy. He apparently had some thoughts about the matter too. "Something to do with that woman and that guy Corson, right? Why would he do this sort of thing, just to get even?"

Morgan didn't answer.

"You don't even know her, do you?"

"Don't have any idea where she is," Morgan said.

"I didn't ask if you know where she is. I asked if you know her."

"Depends on what you mean by know her," Morgan said.

"You hound, you've got yourself involved already."

"Don't worry, we'll find the fuckin' gold," Morgan growled. "But gold or no gold, I'm going to find the son-of-a-bitch who wrinkled my clothes."

"Good," Broom said. "Let's go get something to eat. Maybe we'll think of something else."

"Go ahead. I'll join you in a minute. Just want to check through my stuff and sling the mattress back onto the bed. I'll be right along."

When he was alone in the room, Morgan bolted the door, then checked the fireplace to make sure the intruder had not discovered his hiding place. The bricks appeared undisturbed, looked natural, but Morgan brought the crockery wash basin from the stand on the other side of the room and held it beneath the brick to catch the crumbling mortar. He removed one brick and was relieved to find the leather bag still intact.

Carefully replacing the brick, he again moistened the dusty mortar and tucked it realistically into the cracks.

He stood there wondering where Celia Fair was. He thought about the night before. God, it made him hot just thinking about her. Her silky smooth body and her delicate talented hands. He licked his lips, but tasted only salt and dust.

He wondered how he could get in touch with her. Someone must know. The trouble was, he couldn't take a chance on asking the wrong person.

Dusting out the basin, he poured water in it from the pitcher and washed his face and hands. Then he dried off, went out into the hall, and locked his door.

At the desk downstairs he dropped off the useless skeleton key at the desk. Anybody could get into the room, if you weren't there to slide the bolt on the inside.

Nelly was behind the counter. "Everything all right, Mr. Morgan?"

"Not exactly, Nelly. You see anybody go into my room today while I was gone?"

"No, sir." She looked alarmed. "Has someone been in your room?"

"You might say that. Tore the place all up."

"Oh, dear. It was all right when I made up your bed at ten o'clock, Mr. Morgan." Nelly wrung her hands, her excited voice raised with anxiety. "I'm the only one that was in there. But I didn't muss anything up."

"I know you didn't. But if you get time, you can make up the bed again. I tossed the mattress back on the bed, but the blankets could use help."

"The mattress was off the bed? Wait, I'd better tell Mr. Rowe."

Jeb and Essie Rowe had already come out of an office somewhere behind Nelly. "What's all the fuss about, Nelly?" Essie wanted to know.

"Morgan?" Jeb said.

"Someone got into Mr. Morgan's things, in his room," Nelly said. "I made up his bed this morning. Honest. I didn't move anything. It wasn't a mess then."

Jeb and Essie insisted upon going up with Morgan to see the problem.

"I already put away the bureau drawers and such," Morgan said. "Don't know what they wanted, but someone tore into everything. Not that I have much with me."

"Did they steal something?" Jeb inquired.

"No. I didn't find anything missing. Don't think we need to call in the law or blab it around," Morgan told them. "I wouldn't have mentioned it to Nelly, but I hoped maybe she'd tidy up the bed. I'm not much for bed making."

"Of course, she'll make it right up," Essie said, starting to do the job herself.

Morgan thought they both seemed relieved that he had not wanted to notify the sheriff. He wanted nothing more to do with the damn sheriff. He got the feeling that the Rowes felt the same way.

He thanked them for their help in the matter and went on over to the cafe to meet Hank Broom.

Over their early supper they spoke quietly about the events of the day, glancing around occasionally to make sure no one was near enough to take in their conversation. They reached no conclusions, except that they wanted to find out more about Brant Corson and what he was up to.

They made the rounds of the three saloons to see if Corson was around, but they didn't see him. Morgan got propositions from three different voluptuous bar girls, joked with them, smiled a lot, and rejected all three. He had never felt the need to pay for giving women joy and satisfaction. Better they should pay him. Broom, however, left Morgan to finish his last brandy alone, disappearing with a highly rouged night creature on his arm.

Morgan thought he saw someone watching him from the end of the alley as he made his way back to his hotel. He slowed down to see if they might want to follow along, but they didn't take the bait. He decided he had taken something personally that had nothing to do with him. Probably whoever it was had been watching everyone that went by. There didn't seem to be much else to do in the town except drinking and doxies.

5

After taking his clothes off and cleaning up, Morgan lay on the bed thinking about the things that had taken place. It had been a long day. The Indians, the old timer dead and buried, and Jason Isley. Morgan wondered how much more young Jason knew about the gold than he let on.

But soon Morgan relaxed and began to doze off. In and out of a sort of half sleep, he dreamed about Celia Fair.

He roused suddenly and sat up trying to figure out what had wakened him. It came again. A gentle tapping that made his heart race. Could it be?

He pulled on his pants, buttoning them part way up. Then he stopped short, and before going to the door, took his Bisley Colt out of the holster hanging on the bedpost.

Standing close to the edge of the door, not directly in front of it, he asked, "Yeah? Who is it?"

The tapping came again and a whispered answer. "Celia."

He drew the bolt and opened the door. There she was. He could scarcely believe she had actually reappeared.

This time she wore an ankle-length dark gray

traveling suit that had a white blouse with a
bow at the neck. The jacket of the suit fit her
perfectly, made with long lapels and two
buttons at the pinched in waist. She carried a
plush gray carpet satchel with large yellow
roses and green leaves patterned on the sides.
From one wrist hung a moleskin bag of the sort
women sometimes carried their knitting in. On
her head she wore a bonnet that matched her
suit.

This time Lee Morgan didn't have to be asked
if she could come in. He drew her into the room
immediately, took the carpetbag and set it
aside, and returned the Bisley to its holster on
the bedpost.

"I was thinking about you!" Lee said, taking
hold of her hand.

"Is that why you are practically undressed?"
Her laughtered tinkled out at him, making him
laugh too.

"But you," he held her at arm's length and
looked her over, "you're dressed for travel."

"I'm leaving in the morning. I had to stop and
pick up my bag that I left with you."

Morgan shook his head. A troubled frown
crossed his brow. "You're leaving?"

"Not until morning, Lee." Celia touched his
face with her hand. "I also had to stop because I
wanted to be with you."

He put his arms around her and held her
close to him. Breathing a sigh of relief he told
her, "I want you to be with me. And I want to be
with you."

She drew away momentarily. "You kept my
leather case safe?"

"Of course."

He strode over to the fireplace, shoved the

hearth rug into the right spot to catch the crumbled mortar and once again removed the bricks. He carefully took out the leather bag and dusted it off with a used towel. "There you are. Good as new. And every bit as heavy as it was when you brought it in here."

She took the bag and set it with her other things. "Thank you, Lee. I was sure you would know how to keep it safe for me."

"We picked the right hiding place," Lee told her. "When I got in from some errands yesterday, someone had torn the room apart searching for something."

"For my bag?" Concern clouded Celia's face.

"I don't know what they were looking for." He smiled at her, walked over to the door and made sure the bolt was securely in place. "But they didn't get it. Aren't you going to look in it to make sure it's all right?" He wanted to know what she was carrying.

She picked up the bag again, undid the buckles and opened it. "There they are. It's my jewelry. Heirlooms handed down through my family." She took out a necklace and held it up. It glittered in the lamp light.

Morgan got a quick look over her shoulder before she returned the necklace and closed the bag. Could be a fortune in gems in that bag. She refastened the buckles.

"I brought them with me, because I thought I might have to sell them to help my brother."

"But you didn't have to?" Lee asked her.

"When I got here he was already dead."

"Oh. I'm sorry."

"It's over. I hadn't seen him in a long time." She sighed. "We weren't close. There is nothing I can do about it now."

Celia took off her bonnet and placed it carefully on top of the bags on the floor. She unbuttoned her jacket and hung it on the chair, then sat down and took off her shoes.

She smiled up at Morgan who stood watching her. Her movements, so full of grace, and so sensuous, fascinated and roused him.

As before, she sneaked up under her skirts and slowly, as if teasing him, peeled off the expensive looking stockings, first one and then the other.

"Where are you going on the morning coach?" Morgan asked.

"Salt Lake City. Then on the train. Chicago. Boston." She untied the white bow of her blouse and unbuttoned the buttons, slowly, tantalizingly.

"Why must you go?"

"I have to take care of my father's business." She drew her arms out of the sleeves and dropped the blouse on the chair. "But that's not until tomorrow. Let's not think of those things now."

Morgan stepped closer. He didn't want to think of those things now. In a moment he was helping her out of the rest of her clothes. He shed his pants and finally they embraced. "You feel even better than last night."

"So do you," she murmured.

They kissed, a long tender kiss full of promises. Then Celia's lips found the indentation at the front of his neck, between the ends of his collarbone. Her kiss was feather light and thrilled him. He never knew that spot on him was so responsive.

He bent to kiss her again, but she said. "Come lie down."

They went to the bed, and she told him to lie on his stomach.

"What for?" I can't hold you if I'm lying on my stomach.

"I'll show you," she promised.

He lay down on his stomach as she took a tiny bottle of oil from her moleskin bag and brought it to the bed with her. "Relax," she said. She got on the bed beside him and knelt sitting back on her heels. She leaned over and kissed the middle of his back, sending a shiver up his spine.

In a moment she began to massage his legs with the oil. It felt good. She went from his legs to his back, smoothing the oil with firm strokes from his buttocks to his shoulders, then lighter strokes back down again, her fingers scampering and tickling on the way.

His muscles relaxed, except for one on which he was lying. That organ grew longer and harder.

He felt relaxed and euphoric, yet excited. "Your hands are stronger than they look," he said. "Where did you learn to do that?"

"From my Swedish nanny," she said. "She taught me many things. Do you like it? Your skin is parched from the dry air, and thirsty. It drinks up the oil."

"My skin isn't the only thing that's thirsty. I'm thirsting for you."

After massaging on up to include his shoulders and the back of his neck, she said, "If you're still awake, you may turn over now."

He turned over and she laughed delightedly. "There's something sticking up, here!"

She put aside the little bottle of oil and walked her fingers up his legs, past his excited organ, and all the way up his chest, where she tweeked his nipples.

Lee grabbed her and rolled over with her, pinning her down and kissing her passionately. She returned the kiss making little humming sounds to show her pleasure. She squirmed against him, exciting him even more.

"Put your hands on me," she whispered. "I love to feel your hands on me."

He knew how good her hands felt to him, so he obeyed. While he kissed and suckled her breasts, his hands traversed her smooth skin over her sides, her belly, her thighs. Then he paused. His hand lay there, just touching, making her wait.

Her body made an urging move, tensing, beseeching.

Lee's fingers moved to find the exciting erectile point at the upper tip of her inner labia. He put his thumb on the love button and slowly put a finger into the hole. Adding another finger, he moved first the fingers and then the thumb, and she raised her body trying to take the fingers in farther. The fingers slipped easily, wet with her juices.

Celia stretched a hand trying to reach his groin, but Lee was in the way. He teased. He moved the fingers again, and then the thumb.

"Oh." Her audible sigh. "Oh, please. Please."

He couldn't disappoint a lady, so he raised himself above her, she opened her legs wide, and he thrust his organ into the warm moist place he had prepared for it. She accepted him and moved with passion wanting it deeper and deeper. It seemed to grow even larger after it was inside.

She raised her legs and circled his body,

clutching him tightly as they thrust together, their rhythms sending them to a higher and higher pitch of excitement.

"Now," she cried. "Now. Oh, now."

The release came intensely, lasted forever, and they both moaned in ecstasy, clinging to one another, as her love hole contracted over and over, squeezing his member, making additional thrills chase one after the other up through his body.

When they finally relaxed she stroked his hair and his face and murmured, "You are wonderful, Lee Morgan."

They slept, and when morning came to Morgan, it woke him angry. He found she had gone. She had dressed, picked up her things and gone, while he went on sleeping.

"Damn, woman!" he exclaimed aloud. "How could you go without saying goodbye?" He had wanted to talk her out of it.

Morgan got up, did the morning things, and got dressed. He looked out the window at the street below and saw nothing worth seeing. A couple of riders went by, heading east. Morgan didn't recognize them as anyone he had seen before. A horse was tied at the rail across the street in front of the cafe. There was no stage. He didn't know when it was scheduled to go through Lost Canyon, or if it had gone. He went downstairs.

The night man was still at the desk. He snored loudly. Morgan couldn't think why the Rowes paid him to sit there with his feet up and sleep.

Turning from the desk and going down the hall, he pounded on the door of room six. "Go away." Hank's baritone sounded hoarse this morning.

Morgan went away. He went to the cafe across the street.

There was only one other customer who sat at the counter silently shoveling his eggs into his mouth.

Morgan decided on a table, and the waitress came to him.

When he had ordered breakfast, he asked the sleepy-eyed girl, "What time's the stage today?"

"East or west?" she wanted to know. "This is the day we have two."

"Oh, damn, wouldn't you know." Then he remembered. Celia had said Salt Lake City, Chicago, Boston. "East."

"That one's gone. We got our supplies off it at the crack of dawn. Only a couple people out there." She stood with one hand on the back of the chair opposite Morgan, leaning, ready to stop and chat a while. "Guess there were two or three people already on it, coming through. Didn't stop long enough for them to come over and eat though."

"Who got on from here?" Morgan wanted to know.

"There was an old man, looked like he was going to go back home to die, he was so old. Folks do that, you know. They come out here and they want to go back where they started from, when they get old."

Morgan nodded. "Makes sense."

"I wouldn't want to go back. I grew up here." She poked at her hair, a preening gesture. "I'm going to go clear to the Pacific Ocean one day."

"Who else got on from here?"

"There was a lady, city clothes, so pretty. She stood there talking to a big guy. I don't think he wanted her to go."

"A big guy?" Morgan asked. "Corson? Long hair?"

She nodded. "Ugly."

"Did he hurt her?"

"No, they were just talking. Like I said, I didn't hear anything, but it looked like he wanted her to stay. I know he didn't get on the stage. But she did."

But she did, Morgan thought.

Before Morgan had finished his breakfast, Hank Broom came in and joined him. "You bang on my door earlier? Did you find out something?"

"Sorry," Morgan said.

He had found out nothing. Celia had told him what was in the leather bag. He had loved, and slept, and learned nothing more.

"You look worse than I feel, Morgan," Broom growled. "What the hell's crawled up you?"

"She's gone."

"Damn." Broom exploded. "Just when I was gonna tell you I thought she might be of some use to us. The Isley kid said something about her knowing the old timer. I thought you'd find out something about that."

"I didn't. I let her get away. She came out here to help her brother, but she said he was dead when she got here."

"You think she might have known this Hex Downs character?"

"I don't know."

All Morgan knew was that he hated the idea of Celia having gotten on the stage and leaving town. He hated the idea of Corson talking to her. But at least the son-of-a-bitch hadn't gone with her.

Suddenly another thought hit him. Broom

was right, Jason Isley had said Celia knew the
old man. "My God, you don't think that was her
brother? Jason said Hex Downs went to see the
old man, and Celia went to see the old man. But
she isn't married and her name isn't Downs."

"People can change their names," Broom
said. "Downs might not have been his right
name. Wish you'd have asked her that."

"So do I," Morgan said, feeling even worse.
"Could that have been what Corson wanted
with her? To get her to tell what she knew about
Hex Downs?"

Celia Fair would have given almost anything
to have stayed. Lee Morgan was the first man
she had ever met that she could have remained
with forever. But she had to go back. Her
father's business came first. He had become old
and feeble and, he had signed everything over to
her.

"I've educated you like a man," he told her.
"I've taught you everything about the business.
Now I'd better sign it over, before I get so I can't
sign at all."

So Celia Fair was president and chairman of
the board of Fair Lumber and Ores. Her brother
Hex would have been, but he had gone astray
years ago. Their father had written him off as
the black sheep of the family. "You were always
the smart one, anyhow, my darling Celia," her
father said.

The big Concord stagecoach raced along over
the trail east not making a lot of noise. But like
Celia, everyone inside seemed to be deep in
thought, not wanting to hold conversation with
strangers.

It had been that way coming out, too, but

after many miles, they would loosen up and exchange life stories, destinations, show pictures of children and grandchildren. There were two other women and a man who had been on the stage when it arrived in Lost Canyon. An old man, now apparently sleeping through the bumps and jounces, got on when Celia did.

She had been afraid that Corson wasn't going to let her get on, that he would shake her and drag her away as he had the first time, the day that Lee Morgan had rescued her. At least something wonderful had come out of that frightful experience.

Where would she ever come upon another man so sensitive to a woman's wants and needs? A little shiver went through her just thinking about it. Where would a woman ever find a man who had any idea that a woman could enjoy it, too? A man who would not be shocked to find a decent woman, not a bar girl or a whore, who knew her way around a bed? Lee Morgan, she thought, I hope we meet again.

Suddenly gunfire sounded. The coach swerved and picked up speed, swaying crazily from side to side. The passengers clung to whatever hand-holds they could find. Fear filled the inside of the stage like a fog.

Several more shots were fired, galloping horses' hoofbeats sounded alongside them. Men shouted. The people inside the stage clung to their seats, bouncing as the stage went off the beaten trail.

There were more shots. Then the Concord slowed and stopped.

A man's voice shouted, "Don't do nothing foolish, up there."

A second man added, "Just sit tight and

nobody'll get hurt."

A man with a kerchief tied around his face, so he wouldn't be recognized, stuck his head inside and ordered, "Everybody out."

One of the women began to weep, whimpering, "Oh, no. Oh, no," over and over.

The passengers stepped down one by one. Some of them held their hands up. Someone murmured a prayer. "Hail Mary, Mother of God. . . ."

The old man who boarded in Lost Canyon squeaked, "Don't shoot me, I'm goin' home."

"Nobody's gonna shoot ya, old man," one of the bandits said. He stepped toward them and took Celia by the wrist. "This is what we're after, right here. Where's your bag, lady?"

Celia tried to pull away, then not wanting to get someone shot, pointed to the top of the stage. "The one with the roses. You can have it."

The driver threw it down. "Can't help you, lady. We got orders not to get ourselves killed."

"Smart." The bandit holding onto Celia's wrist picked up the bag.

His partner, holding a rifle, rasped, "Why can't we get a little bonus here?" He poked at one woman's purse. "Pick up a little extra cash, some trinkets."

"Shut up, Axel. We'll take only what was ordered." He waved the passengers back into the stage. "You can go now."

As soon as the others were inside, the driver whipped up the horses and tore away leaving only a cloud of dust and Celia in the hands of the two gunmen.

"What do you want of me?" she asked, trying to control her voice.

The man with the vise grip on her wrist said,

"Just followin' orders." He put his pistol in its holster.

The other rammed his rifle into the holder at the side of his saddle and mounted up. "Want the little lady to ride with me?"

"Get back down here and tie up her hands, stupid."

"I'm not going to run away from you on foot in the desert without any water," Celia said in a reasonable tone, sounding much more calm than she really was. "Where are we going?"

"Shut up," her captor said.

The one called Axel dismounted again and said, "How's she gonna hang on with her hands tied up?"

His partner relented. "Okay, just put her on behind me."

The other man got on his horse and Axel cupped his hands for Celia to put her foot in. "Come on. Unless you want me to grab you and hoist you on."

She complied. There was nothing else to do. In a moment she was on the horse with her skirts hoisted clear above her knees and one of her stockings ruined in the process. She wondered whether she would live to see another pair, or anything else.

Axel gave an appreciative leer at her shapely leg, fastened her carpetbag to his saddle horn, and mounted up. They started back in the direction from which she had come on the stage.

They rode in silence for a long time. The sun beat down on Celia's head, the bonnet helped shade her face, but it made her feel hotter than if the breeze created by trotting along had been allowed to blow through her hair. Perspiration ran between her breasts. The rough ride and sitting in the awkward position behind her captor, having to hang on to him around his waist, made her legs and back ache. She was so uncomfortable she could scarcely feel the fear she knew was inside her. There was no one to save her this time.

Had that loathesome Corson spoken so quietly to her earlier just to point her out to these men, and then sent them to take her? What was going to happen to her?

At least they didn't have the right bag. Her leather case had her name and address on it. The stage company would hold it for her. Her jewels and Hex's note would go on to Salt Lake City to wait for her. If she lived to claim them.

When Celia thought she could no longer bear it, they reached a ranch. The men approached an outbuilding and dismounted. As her captor lifted her down, she practically fell into his hands.

"Better get this little lady a drink of water."

"Me too," the other one said and set off toward a windmill some distance away.

Celia sat on an old bench beside the shack and removed her bonnet. In a few minutes Axel returned with a tin cup of water. He spilled it on her skirt while handing it to her. She didn't care. She felt completely hopeless by this time, but the water revived her. She said, "Thank you," automatically, then wondered why.

They took her inside the shack and pointed to an open steamer trunk. Her heart beat madly. What were they going to do with her? Bury her alive! She would die.

"Get in and lie down," barked the one who always took charge.

She stood still shaking her head. Celia was not a woman who cried easily, nor was she easily frightened. But tears welled into her eyes and terror gripped her insides. She started to scream, but the man's dirty hand stopped her. "Nobody around to hear you, anyhow."

"Hey." He took hold of her arm. "It won't be for long. Nothing's gonna happen to you. We don't want anybody to see you come back to town. If you're going to raise cain, we can always dope you up. Or hit you over the head."

There was an old quilt on the bottom of the trunk. The man urged her forward with a grip on both her arms.

She made a slight move to fight back, but he lifted her easily into the trunk and pushed her so that she lay down on her side, curled up. "I won't be able to breathe."

"You'll be able to breathe, but it'll go hard on you if you make a lot of noise before we get there."

He closed the cover and she heard the hasp click down and something push through to secure it. She realized she was holding her breath. She started to breathe again with a sob.

They picked up the trunk and moved it, setting it on something, possibly a wagon, which then began to move. It was a sore and bumpy ride. It went on and on forever. It hurt her shoulder and her hip. Her head drummed with pain. The trunk was getting stuffy. She was going to die after all. She started to call out. She made only a small noise, but she kicked with her heel at the back of the trunk.

The wagon stopped. The lid opened. She started to sit up and tell them she couldn't breathe. Suddenly a rag was clamped over her face. She tried to fight it off.

Chloroform was the last word she thought of.

She woke dizzy, nauseated and tied to a chair. There was a gag in her mouth so she couldn't speak.

She tried to take slower breaths so she wouldn't be sick with the horrid rag bound into her mouth. She stared around trying to see where she was. The lace curtained windows across the room showed the dimming light of late evening.

Lace curtains? The hotel! The same hotel where Lee Morgan had a room? It must be. She was in the hotel in Lost Canyon.

She must try to get her senses clear, so she could think. She must find a way to bring help.

Someone put a key in the lock and opened the door. It was the bossy kidnaper. "Axel's bringing you something to eat. Then there's someone who'll want to talk to you."

Celia suddenly realized, with a shock of fear, that these men had pulled the bandanas down from their faces as soon as the stage had left her with them in the desert. They had not cared from then on that she could see their faces. She didn't know who they were, but she could see them. They would kill her at the end of whatever they were after, so she wouldn't recognize them later. She was going to die.

"We're gonna take this out of your mouth. If you scream, I'll fix you so you'll really have something to scream about. You got that?"

Celia nodded.

He took the gag out of her mouth. He untied her hands. Axel came with soup and bread and coffee. "I didn't spill much," he said.

She took a sip of the coffee, at least getting

the rag taste out of her mouth. She thought she would be sick, but somehow managed not to be. "Why am I here?"

"Somebody wants to see you."

"Could I wash my face?" Her hands shook so she had trouble holding the coffee cup. She set it down. She couldn't think well enough to know what to do. If they untied her feet from the chair legs, would she be able to find a way to get away? Or would they put her back to sleep?

6

The sleepy-eyed waitress came to take Broom's order for breakfast, but she directed her smile at Morgan. "Can I get you anything more, Mr. Morgan?"

"Maybe more coffee."

"Yes. Yes, right away. Sorry, I should have refilled your cup sooner." The flustered waitress hurried away for the pot.

"You never fail to charm them all, Morgan." Broom directed a sly look at his friend. "Especially Celia Fair?"

"I didn't charm Celia enough. She left."

"Think she could be Down's sister? If she is, there's a good chance she knows something."

"And she's taking what she knows back to Boston."

"Maybe she doesn't care about the gold or maybe. . . ." Broom frowned. "Maybe she didn't know why her brother needed help, if he was her brother."

The waitress flirted openly with Morgan when she refilled his cup. Then, as if it were an afterthought, poured more coffee into Broom's half full cup.

"Thanks for the great service, Florrie," Broom said. "Now I'll have to put more sugar in." He laughed. "And I won't know how much, you've got me all mixed up."

The burly man over at the counter finished his breakfast and paid. She thanked him profusely for the generous tip. "Just want to be friendly, little lady," he said and eyed the young girl from her slim waist to her neck.

Morgan watched, amused. She was a friendly kid, probably not yet seventeen. Her eyes reflected a kind of loneliness not unfamiliar to him.

Morgan's glance roamed around the restaurant. The six other tables, covered with worn oil cloth, were empty except that each held a can of condensed milk, punctured with two holes, and shakers of pepper and salt. No one sat at the counter now.

Florrie leaned against the jam of the door leading to the kitchen, where now and then a dish clattered as if it were being stacked with others to dry.

Morgan sipped at his coffee waiting for Broom to finish eating. Not much of a breakfast crowd. He dragged out his Waterbury. Nearly nine o'clock. Probably most had come and gone.

Through the glass in the door, he saw Corson approach. Automatically he felt for his Bisley Colts, then relaxed. He noticed Broom did the same. Morgan chided himself. They were both getting jumpy. That was a fast way to get yourself killed. Corson had as much right to come into the cafe as anyone else.

Corson came into the restaurant and slowly, it seemed to Morgan, closed the door behind himself. Damn, he was an ox of a man, and the anger that screwed up his ugly face was not reassuring.

Corson came straight toward their table. Like cracking a whip, he snaked his forty-five from its holster and pointed it at Morgan. Lee heard Florrie start to cry out, the end of her cry muffled, as if she had put her hand over her mouth as she retreated to the kitchen.

Corson leveled his gun at Morgan's head. "Celia said she left her bag with a friend. She didn't have a lot of friends. Ole is dead, that leaves you. I want it."

Morgan's mind whirled. Had Celia told Corson that when she left this morning? What if Corson was her brother? No, she'd said her brother was dead. If she told him she'd left the bag, why hadn't he come on to Morgan sooner, like in his room right after the stage left? There, he wouldn't have had an audience. "Is that why you tore up my room yesterday?"

"I didn't tear up your damn room. That bag is your death warrant unless you turn it over."

Corson had the drop on them. Morgan tried to look nonchalant, but he sure didn't feel that way. "I don't have any bag. She probably took it with her when she left on the morning coach."

He saw Corson's finger tighten on the trigger. "Now, you son-of-a-bitch," he barked, "I want that bag!"

Lee felt Broom tense beside him, felt the miniscule movement of his hand toward his gun. Broom was fast, but didn't he realize he couldn't outdraw a man with a forty-five already in his hand?

Corson must have seen Broom's movement. He aimed the gun at Broom's head. "Try it and I'll splash your brains all over the floor."

Broom tried it. Two simultaneous shots exploded. Morgan dropped to the floor and whipped out his Bisley. Corson had been right about Broom. The forty-five had blown a hole in Broom's brow and splattered the back of his head all over the floor behind him.

Morgan raised his Bisley Colts to gun the killer down.

He squinted at Corson in disbelief. Corson, shocked surprise on his face, clutched at a neat round hole in his chest, just over his heart, and slowly sank to the floor.

Broom's hand still gripped his pistol, only halfway out of the holster.

Morgan rolled, landed crouched, but on his feet. "Who the hell. . . ?"

The only other person in sight stood at the kitchen door, a weapon still in his hand. "Jason!" Lee bellowed. "Put that damned thing away."

"He was going to kill you," Jason babbled. "He wanted to kill both of you."

Outside people yelled. "Shooting. There's a shooting in the cafe."

Morgan sprinted toward Jason. The door to the cafe opened slowly, as if the person on the other side didn't want to be a victim too. Morgan grabbed Jasons gun and tossed it underhand. It thudded almost noiselessly into the kitchen garbage bucket. "Keep your mouth shut," he ordered.

Jason backed away, apparently still in awe of what he had done.

Morgan went back to the table, bent over and jerked Broom's gun from its holster and let it drop on the floor. He and Broom went back a long way. Later, there would be time for remembering. Right now he had to convince the sheriff of a downright lie.

Corson groaned.

He wasn't quite dead, but he soon would be. Morgan stooped down beside him. "Where's the gold, Corson. It won't do you any good now."

"Doctor," Corson rasped. Blood trickled from the corner of his mouth.

"You're dying, Corson, you know you are. Maybe your partners arranged it, whoever sent you in after me. Tell me where it is, and I'll see that the greedy bastards don't get it."

Apparently Brant Corson realized it was over. "Don't know." His next words were almost inaudible, but Morgan leaned close and caught them. "Celia knows," he said. Then his eyes rolled up, and Corson was staring blankly at the ceiling of the cafe.

Sheriff Bert Tyler, brandishing a bulky revolver, pushed the spectators aside and plunged into the cafe. "What's going on in here?" he demanded.

Morgan holstered his gun. "Guess they were enemies from way back," he said calmly.

The sheriff looked at Broom without flinching, then down at Corson. "He never was very smart," he said.

By then a dozen townspeople crowded into the cafe. At the kitchen door, Florrie, the waitress, her eyes round with shock, stood beside Jason. Morgan caught Jason's eye and gave him a silent warning to keep out of it.

The sheriff holstered his gun. "Any witnesses?"

"Just me, I guess," Morgan said. "You know Broom was fast. Corson should have watched him closer. I thought Corson had him beat."

The sheriff pointed a finger at Morgan. "You seem to be right in the middle of every killing lately. I told you to get out of town. If I see you again, I'll run you out." He paused. "Or maybe I'll run you in. You got no proof you didn't do it, if you're the only witness."

"My gun hasn't been fired." He held it out in the palm of his hand.

The sheriff felt of the barrel, shrugged and turned to a couple of the townspeople who still stared at the dead bodies on the floor. "You two," he said, indicating two rough-looking men nearby. "Get these bodies out of here and over to the undertaker." Then he turned and left.

When he was out of sight, Jason rushed over to Morgan. "I . . . I never did that before," he stammered. "I never killed. . . ."

Morgan shushed him, then looked down at Broom. "Old Hank should have known better than try to draw when Corson had the drop on us."

"He was trying to save your life."

"I know. He's done it before."

Morgan pushed Jason back into the kitchen. "Get your gun, you may need it. Where did you learn to shoot like that?"

Jason dug his gun out of the trash can and wiped it off before holstering it. "Gramps taught me. He believed everybody should know how to shoot straight. Do you think Corson intended to kill you?"

"He looked like it."

"I think he was really after Broom," Jason said. "Anybody who knew Broom knew he could be reckless if he was provoked and there was bad blood between those two. I think Corson wanted to kill Broom ever since he got to town."

"Or without Broom to back me up, maybe

Corson figured I'd get out of town."

"Think the sheriff meant what he said?"

"Guess I'll stay away from my room at the hotel for a little while, just in case the sheriff or anybody else gets any ideas. You got a room here in town I can use while I get my thoughts straightened out?"

"Sure. I've got the back room here at the cafe, come on." Jason led Lee to a storeroom behind the kitchen. One small window let in a little sunlight, showing a neatly made cot and boxes stacked to make shelves for his clothes. "It's not much, but I get it as part of my pay for working in the kitchen."

Morgan sat down on the edge of the cot. The blanket was clean, and he noticed the floor had been swept. Gramps had taught Jason more than how to shoot a gun and read a book.

With Broom and Celia gone, Morgan thought, he had no friends in Lost Canyon. He'd have to watch his back every minute. Maybe he should move on. But he could sure use that gold if he could find it, and he still hadn't found the son-of-a-bitch who ransacked his room.

Jason sat on the one chair in the room, which looked like a spare from the restaurant. Morgan noticed him squeezing his hands nervously. He couldn't leave the kid alone. If the sheriff got hold of him, he'd break and admit to the shooting, sure as hell, wrought up as he was.

Florrie burst through the door. "Corson's brother Joe, and three of his ranch hands just rode in to town. They're at the undertaker's place."

Jason jumped to his feet and shoved a worn felt hat on his head. "I'll face them. I'll tell big Joe how it was."

"And you'll get shot down." Morgan gripped Florrie's shoulders. "We're leaving by the back door. Corson's brother will be over here. Stick to the story that Corson and Broom shot each other, if anybody asks. Can you do that? If you don't, it's all up for Jason."

Florrie's gaze flew to Jason. Morgan wasn't surprised at the warmth it displayed. "I can do it." She pushed Jason and Morgan toward the back door. "Stay behind the buildings to the livery and nobody will see you."

Jason hesitated. The front door of the cafe burst open, and Florrie ran to serve them. "Where's the tall guy who saw the shooting? The bastard who said Broom shot my brother. He's a damn liar! He's the one Brant was after."

Morgan shoved Jason out the back door. "Come on," he growled. "There are times when honesty is not the best policy."

Once outside, Jason's hesitation vanished. "They think you did it." He lowered his head to stay out of sight through the back window of the saloon, and ran ahead of Morgan to the end of the row of buildings and across the street. They found cover again behind the buildings on that side until they got to the stables.

"Let them think it."

Inside the stable, Willie, the ten year old with the dog smiled broadly when Jason and Morgan came in. "You gonna teach me how to use the whip today?"

"Not today. We've got to leave as fast as we can." Morgan stooped down and talked earnestly to the boy. "If anyone asks you if you've seen us, will you tell them we haven't been here?"

The boy nodded solemnly. "I won't tell." Then

he scurried around helping them saddle up. "I promise I won't tell, no matter what, and Pa's not here. I'm in charge."

Jason patted the boy's dog before he and Morgan cautiously led their horses out the rear door.

"We can't go up to the cabin, not with close to four miles of open ground to cover before we get to the timber." Morgan pointed. "How about those trees? What's beyond them?"

"The quarry. There's caves up there."

Without further comment, Morgan spurred his horse into a gallop and in minutes they were within cover of the live oaks. Then he let Jason lead the way.

They followed rusty iron tracks, obviously put in to cart rock down to the town, for close to half a mile through the trees, then they stopped on the rim of the quarry. Endless piles of broken rock littered both sides of the stretch of tramway. At the end of the tracks three holes, that appeared to be caves, offered them cover.

Morgan reached for his canteen and shook it. "The kid must have filled them. Is he a good friend of yours?"

"There's not much to do evenings after the cafe closes. We play cards some. And we went rabbit hunting together a couple of times."

They headed for the far cave. The horses' hooves raised an acrid dust. Morgan could smell it and taste it on his lips. "How long since you've been up here?"

"Been a while. I used to come and watch them blast rock from the side of the hill. The town built a new jail with the rocks, but the mortar didn't hold and two men escaped. That about ended the rock business."

Jason led the way to the mouth of the cave, dismounted and led his horse inside. Morgan followed. "This is the deepest one," Jason said. "It will keep the horses out of sight."

Inside, Morgan stared uneasily at the rock walls and ceiling. Several long cracks suggested danger of a cave-in, especially if they were disturbed by gunfire. And Morgan had no doubt that Corson's brother and his three ranch hands would come looking for them. They hadn't covered their trail.

At least Jason and Morgan had time on their side. It would take a while for Joe Corson to figure out where they had gone.

They sat down on the floor of the cave, far enough in to be out of sight, but still able to see any approaching riders.

Jason fiddled nervously with his gun, making sure it was fully loaded, checking it again. "I never killed a man before. I feel creepy all over. Does it ever go away?"

Morgan leaned back against the wall of the cave and perched his tan Stetson on his knee. "Sometimes it never goes away, especially if you feel you made a mistake."

"Did I make a mistake when I shot Corson? He would have killed you, too. I'm sorry about Broom. He was your friend from a long time ago, wasn't he?"

"He saved my life once." Morgan smiled remembering. "I hung around his place for a spell after that. But yes, that was a very long time ago."

Morgan sighed and was quiet for a while. Then he began again. "He got a gang together and they held up stage coaches and robbed a bank or two. That's when he wouldn't see me any more. Told me to be on my way. I might have joined his gang, but he wouldn't let me, said I was too young. Said I was too soft for killing."

"Are you?" Jason asked.

"Not when it's necessary."

Morgan dragged out his Waterbury and checked the time. Nearly two o'clock. It was cool in the cave, so he couldn't tell it was mid-afternoon. He didn't want to talk any more about Hank Broom, it made his gut hurt. Soft? Broom's big heart, standing up for a friend again, did him in.

Suddenly Morgan stiffened, every sense on alert. "Horses," he whispered. "Do you think Willie talked?"

"Not unless his pa beat him half to death."

"Is his pa a friend of Sheriff Tyler?"

"No, he hates him, but he's scared of him, and he hasn't got the guts to stand up to him."

Felipe, Jason's horse whinnied. Jason jumped to his feet and clapped his hand on the horse's muzzle. "Quiet, boy," he soothed. Felipe quieted down.

The sound of hoofbeats came closer. Morgan took the Spencer rifle out of his saddle boot. Guns cocked, Morgan and Jason took places just inside the mouth of the cave.

The riders, Joe Corson and three of his ranch hands, stopped at the rim of the quarry. Their horses pawed the sand, eager to advance. The men talked, but there was no way Morgan or Jason could hear what they said from at least a hundred yards away.

The riders separated, two taking one side of the quarry, the other two advancing along the rock wall of the other side. Once again, Morgan glanced at the long cracks in the rocks inside their cave.

Jason noticed. "We could get buried alive, couldn't we?"

Morgan nodded. "I suppose. Don't fire unless you have to."

"Maybe they won't know we're here."

"They know. All they need to do is look at the fresh prints in the sand. But they obviously don't know which cave we're in."

"This is the only one big enough to hide the horses."

"We're not sure they know that." Morgan didn't want the boy to panic. He was in a bad enough state over his first kill. "We'll just be quiet."

They watched two men dismount and creep to the edge of the far cave. Gunfire exploded. They were testing.

Lee and Jason remained quiet.

The two men on the opposite side of the quarry galloped along the rock face toward their friends. Morgan and Jason edged back out of sight as they passed within ten feet of them. The four men disappeared into the other cave.

Jason moved back into place to see better. "Wonder what they're doing in there." he said softly. "Maybe they're looking for the gold."

"Was Brant Corson that close to his brother?"

"Joe's a ranch owner. Brant worked for him sometimes, but mostly Brant hung around town, around Sheriff Tyler's office."

"Brant knew about the gold, so the sheriff probably does, too. If the others who know have figured out that you know, you better watch yourself."

Two of the men emerged from the far cave, then the other two followed. They walked, kind of bunched together, toward the mouth of the second cave.

"They're getting too close," Morgan whispered. "Aim carefully, so we don't get too much return fire. Don't shoot to kill, unless you have to. Get them in the leg or thigh or the hand, just enough to send them running."

Morgan raised his Spencer rifle. Jason took careful aim with a hand gun. "Now," Morgan ordered. A volley of shots exploded, as fast as the two could fire.

None of the men had time to draw, they were busy hopping around, holding a shot-up foot off the ground, or cursing and grabbing a shoulder. Only Joe Corson, who brought up the rear, appeared not to be hit.

The three injured men dropped to the ground, all trying to hold their injuries and draw their guns at the same time. These were ranch hands, not expert gunnies. For several seconds, Joe Corson crouched behind them. When he realized his men could not protect him, he attempted to make the long dash for the cave they had just left.

Morgan placed two rifle shots against the rocks in front of Joe. He skidded to a stop. He looked around frantically for cover. There was none. He grabbed his horse, mounted and leaned in over it. The horse moved fast. Lee held his fire. From that distance and a fast moving target, he would probably injure only the horse. He didn't want to do that.

When the three ranch hands saw Joe heading out, they scrambled for their horses as best they could, holstered their weapons and rode away.

Jason leaned against the wall of the cave and let his breath out in a long sigh of relief. "Think they'll be back?"

"No. I don't think Joe Corson is anxious to get himself killed even to avenge his brother. He moved pretty fast out of here." Morgan glanced at the sun. Mid afternoon. "I think we better get out of here too, before somebody decides to tear up my room again."

"Your room? When?"

"Before we got back from Gramp's cabin."

"What did they take?"

"They didn't find what they were looking for."

Jason frowned. "Could it have been the same person who killed Gramps? They tore up his cabin looking for something, you know."

"It all boils down to one thing," Morgan said. "The gold. A lot of people in this town seem to know about it, including you. If we're going to catch whoever killed Gramps, you have to tell me everything you know about the gold."

They were through the trees and the town of Lost Canyon lay ahead, before Jason finally spoke. "I don't know how your friend, Broom, found out about it, but Gramps told me some gold had been stolen off a train near Sacramento. He read it in the newspaper. He gets them . . . I mean, *got* them late, after his friend in town has read 'em. Gramps said he figured Hex Downs was the robber that got away."

"But he didn't turn him in to the sheriff. I thought Gramps was a law abiding citizen."

"Nobody trusts Sheriff Tyler, especially not the ranchers. They've been trying to get him to leave, but he won't go. And nobody wants to go up against his fast gun, or his cronies." Jason shrugged. "So I guess he'll just stay until he decides to leave."

"That's it? That's all you know?"

Jason was silent. Morgan had the feeling that although Jason liked him, he had not yet decided whether to trust him.

"Well, the sheriff wants to see me out of town." As they rode into the main street, Morgan headed for the livery stable. "I have to go see the undertaker. It's over at the furniture store isn't it?"

Jason nodded. Then as they dismounted, he stood close to Morgan and said. "I think Gramps knew things he didn't tell me. He thought it could be dangerous for me."

It could be dangerous for anybody who knew too much. Suddenly, Morgan was glad that Celia Fair had gotten out of town.

7

Morgan found the undertaker at the funeral parlor connected to the furniture store. Called Goodrun, he was a long lean old fellow in a black suit who spoke in a monotone. Morgan talked with Goodrun about the proper arrangements for his friend's burial.

"Hank Broom's been in town before for different spells. He's acquainted, that is, *was* acquainted with more people here than I am," Morgan said. "Suppose some of them might want to know."

"They'll know," the old undertaker said.

Morgan returned to the cafe.

Jason had been watching for his return and came out of the kitchen to meet him. "You aren't leavin' town, are you? On account of Hank Broom gettin' killed and Corson's brother coming after us?"

"Hadn't planned to just yet," Morgan growled, and in an even lower voice, he drawled, "For one thing, that Sheriff Tyler is too eager to have me go. Outside of him and the Corson gang, the rest of the townspeople I've met so far don't seem to find me objectionable. Believe I'll hang around awhile and figure out why the sheriff feels the way he does."

Jason drew himself up as tall as possible and grinned broadly. "I was hopin' you'd say that!"

"Yeah?"

"I want to help you find the you-know-what." Jason glanced around to see who was close enough to hear.

"Well, I suppose that would be all right. If you think I need help."

"The way things around here been going, you'll need somebody protectin' your butt, Jason declared. "Or at least someone who knows the territory."

"You have a point there. When do you get through working today?" Morgan wanted to know.

"I'm all caught up for now. I might have to come back." They sat at one of the tables in the almost empty restaurant. The young waitress, Florrie, brought them steaming cups of coffee and smiled sweetly at Jason.

When she had left them alone, Morgan asked, "What do you know about it anyhow, Jason?"

"You mean the gold? Nothing."

"Not just the gold, but all the people that might have had something to do with it. Might have had their hands on it or wanted to get their hands on it." Morgan pushed his hat to the back of his head. "Hex Downs came to see your Gramps. Celia Fair went to see your Gramps. What did they have to do with each other?"

"Hex was dead by the time his sister got here."

"His sister." Morgan nodded thoughtfully. "I wondered about that. She said something about coming to help her brother and that he was dead by the time she got out here. She just failed to say who her brother was." He gazed out the window for a long moment.

People who went by outside slowed to stare in, as if the news of the shooting had made its way around town.

Finally Morgan continued speculating. "It's possible that Hex Downs told the old man something and the old man in turn told Celia."

"I don't know," Jason insisted. "Gramps never said."

"No, but Corson obviously thought she knew something about it, because that was the last thing the bastard said. With his dying breath."

"It must be true, if he said it when he was dying," Jason said earnestly. "They always tell the truth then."

"I suppose." Morgan stood up. "When can we go back out to your cabin? We've got to see if there's something hidden out there."

Morgan paid for the breakfasts he and Broom had eaten before the shooting.

"I knew you wouldn't forget," the waitress told him. "I'm sorry about your friend. But I can't say the same about the other one."

"Right."

"Minute I saw him come in, before I even knew he had his gun in his hand, I went right out to the kitchen and told Jason."

Morgan nodded.

" 'There's gonna be trouble,' I told him."

"Appreciate that, Florrie," Morgan said. "Maybe you saved my life, who knows. You and Jason, here. If he hadn't got Corson, I might have been next."

"And I appreciate you not saying anything different to the sheriff, too," Jason put in.

"With Sheriff Tyler, it's just as well to let him think what he thinks," Florrie said scornfully.

"He's never been known to be right, yet, has he?"

Jason gave Florrie a shy grin and followed Morgan out of the cafe. They stood in the sun in front of the building for a moment. "Think we could ride out there some time today? Your Gramps could have had the gold stashed away for Hex Downs all along. Only nobody has looked in the right place yet."

"I've been thinking about that, Mr. Morgan."

"Drop the mister, kid."

"All right, uh, Lee. Anyhow, what I thought was that Gramps didn't have the gold. But he might have known where it was. He could have left some kind of a clue. He was a clever old guy." Jason smiled remembering. "We used to play games. He'd make up games for learning stuff, like 'rithmetic games and spelling games. And if I couldn't get the answers right off, he'd give me clues to help me figure things out."

"Sounds like a possibility all right. When can we go back out there?" Morgan clapped the boy on the shoulder. "I don't want to go prowling around *your* place all by myself."

"I'll get the time off. I haven't taken any time for a while. When you want to go?"

"I'll go over to the hotel, get my gear and meet you at the livery stable, if you're sure you can fix it up to get off work."

As they stood there, two riders left town at a canter heading northwest.

"You know those two?" Morgan wanted to know.

Jason shook his head. "Could be some more of Corson's brother's ranch hands. The Corson ranch is closest one to town. But it's east of town, opposite of what they were heading. No, I don't know who they are."

"Didn't look like any of that lot that were after us," Morgan commented. "Besides, those sorry s.o.b.s need time to heal up."

They parted and Morgan went over to the hotel. As he started for his room, Essie Rowe called to him from behind the reception desk. "See you for a minute, Mr. Morgan?"

"Sure." He went over to the desk and took off his Stetson. "What can I do for you, Mrs. Rowe?"

"I heard about Hank Broom."

Morgan nodded. "He owing some on his room when he died?" Morgan reached into his pocket. He probably had barely enough left to pay his own way.

"No, no! It isn't that," Essie said. "Goodness, no. We wouldn't think of. . . ."

"With the number of people passin' away around here lately, you could go broke not thinking of that," he told her.

Although there was no one else in the hotel lobby, Essie lowered her voice. "He left something for you."

"He did?"

"When he first checked in, he left this package." From under the counter, she drew a thin packet wrapped in butcher paper and tied with a string. "He said if anything happened to him, we were to give it to you. So I wrote your name on it and here it is."

Morgan took the package. It had his name on the outside, in Essie Rowe's neat penmanship. "Thank you."

"He must have been real sure of your coming, because it was before you even got here. We hadn't even met you. He told us your name and

said you'd be here, and if anything ever
happened to him, you were to have it.''

"Yes, ma'am. Will you be needing any help
with getting his things out of his room?''

"No. He had a steamer trunk and it's
addressed to his papa, the Reverend Mr. Broom
in I-ow-ay. So we'll send it on the Wells Fargo,
whenever they come through. Probably
Tuesday week.''

Morgan nodded and picked up his hat from
the counter.

"Don't usually have people to bring trunks
with them,'' Essie chatted on. "But another man
came in with one just yesterday. Had a friend
helpin' him lug it in. Looked to be heavy.''

"Maybe he brought his books along. Books
are heavy,'' Morgan said. "I knew a professor
fellow once, lugged his books wherever he
went.''

"He didn't look like any professor.'' Essie
shook her head. "But I'm glad this one had help
with his. Don't want Jeb's back going bad on
him again.''

Morgan nodded, put on his hat and went
upstairs to his room.

After bolting the door, he sat down on the
edge of the bed and untied the string, laid back
the butcher paper, and found bank notes. Hank
had left him a wad of money.

There was a message on lined paper in Hank's
labored scrawl. *This is so's you won't of come
for nuthin in case somethin hapens to me.*

Hank was not big on spelling. But he had certainly called it right. Something had happened
to him.

*If you go ahead for the gold, watch out for a
guy named Corson.*

Corson was dead, Morgan thought. But then Hank had written the note before that. He had written the note before he even knew that Corson would be the first man Morgan would tangle with when he came into the damn town.

Folding the bank notes along with Hank's message, he shoved them deep into a side pants pocket. There was enough there to keep him going for a while, and maybe even to take care of a decent burial for Broom. Now, Morgan thought, if he and Jason could just get close to that damned gold!

Morgan picked up his black snake whip and his rifle and headed for the livery stable. The sun was high in the sky and there wasn't a cloud anywhere.

Jason was already there, horse saddled, waiting for him. "Don't have to go in again until late tomorrow. I brought along some grub." He patted a saddlebag.

"Good. Let's go." Morgan got the bay gelding ready and mounted up.

Riding up to the cabin, Morgan kept a sharp look out. He didn't relish the thought of another run-in of the type he'd had making the trip with Hank Broom. It didn't take them as long to get there, since they had no Indian fights or other trouble along the way. But as they neared the property, they found fresh hoof prints on the trail.

"Has there been more traffic along here than I remembered?" Morgan asked. "Or am I skittery?"

"Somebody's up there right now," Jason said. "I can tell by the way Felipe acts."

"You've had that horse a long time, I'll bet," Morgan guessed. "When you have a horse a long time, he'll talk to you. So I'd believe the horse.''

They slowed and peered through the trees. Although they saw no one, Jason dismounted. "Let's go round back."

Morgan agreed and they led their horses for a way, then looped their reins around a couple of low limbs, continuing without the mounts. Morgan took his rifle with him. Jason had one of his revolvers in hand.

They crept quietly through the trees being careful not to make unnecessary noise in the underbrush. About a hundred yards out in the timber, as they came even with the back corner of the building, they could see the shed and the area at the rear of the cabin.

Behind the cabin were two men. They appeared to be the two that Morgan had seen riding out earlier. One of them was about to climb in through the rear window.

"Hold it, right there," Jason shouted.

He was premature with his demand. They were still a little too far away. However, the startled man fell back out of the window. The other one ran for his horse.

Jason fired, although he was out of range. The man on the ground scrambled away crabwise, trying to regain his feet. Morgan took aim with the rifle. He got off one shot when he realized that Jason was running toward the cabin.

"Get down, you fool," Morgan yelled and took another shot at the man who had dropped to the ground still scrambling.

The intruder finally made it to his feet and as he started to run, he turned and fired once before he got to his horse. His shot was short and went wide as well.

Morgan saw red spurt from the man's

shoulder. I may have winged him, he thought.

Jason ran for the cabin, firing and yelling. But the two men had already reached their horses and made good their escape around the corner of the building and out of sight down the trail on the other side.

Morgan strolled on up to the back door of the cabin looking disgusted.

"Oh, well," Jason said, kicking at the dirt with the toe of his boot. "I've shot enough guys for today anyhow."

Morgan relented and grinned at him. "I like a man that can laugh at himself when he makes a bone-head play like that."

"I guess I should have been closer," Jason admitted sheepishly.

"At least we came on them before they got in. So they didn't get anything."

"Probably took them a long time to find their way," Jason said. "I'm glad it did."

They went back to where they had tied their horses and brought them around behind the shed where there was a water barrel and fresh grazing.

Jason said nothing the whole time. Morgan could see his mind was busy with memories of Gramps and their years together, so he let the silence be.

When they'd taken the saddles off and put their gear inside the lean-to, they went into the cabin. Everything was as they had left it the day before.

It was almost nightfall by the time they had gone through everything in the cabin again, searched the shed, and come up empty.

"I can't understand it," Jason said finally. "I thought sure there would be some kind of sign, some clue."

"How did your Gramps usually make these clues when he was teaching you stuff?"

"Oh, he'd draw a picture, something like that." Jason's face took on a faraway look again. "Sometimes in summer, like it was today, we'd be out under the trees with a breeze ruffling the book pages and the papers."

"You studied in the summer?"

"Sure. Gramps said it was always good to be ahead when the next schoolmarm showed up. And he never let me give up." He shrugged, as if trying to relate to Morgan instead of Gramps. Finally he straightened. "Well, we don't have to give up either. Let's have something to eat and stay here tonight."

"Sure. We can go out and see that the horses have a good place for the night. And maybe we can have a look around on the outside, before it gets too dark."

They went out and while Jason took care of the horses and the mule, Morgan walked all the way around the cabin, admiring the way it was built. There were marks that showed where the logs had been checked to set together. Nicks and scratches and chisel gouges that had lasted through the years. Then he found something that had nothing to do with the way the logs went together and although it was not that fresh, neither had it weathered for years.

He studied it for a moment, then called Jason over. "What's this supposed to be?"

Jason frowned and ran his fingers over the carving in the wood. "I never saw that before. Done with a knife. Like you'd carve your initials in a tree."

"Looks recent. But not today or yesterday."

"Done since I lived here."

"What is it supposed to be? Can you tell?"

"It's like an Indian picture. It could be a hill. No, a rainbow. With an arrow at one end," Jason said.

"And a tepee," Morgan finished for him.

"At the end of a rainbow, there's supposed to be a pot of gold." Jason jumped up and down. "It's the clue. I bet Gramps put it there after Hex Downs was killed. Wish he'd a told me."

"From here, the arrow's pointing to the northwest. Is it supposed to be aiming at the tepee?"

"Maybe toward the Indian camp," Jason said.

"Those Indians Broom and I had a run-in with?" Morgan thought they would not have a hell of a lot of luck if they decided the gold was in one of those tepees.

"Gramps was friendly with the Chief. Gramps always got along fine with the Indians. Especially with Chief Greatfoot."

Jason pulled out provisions he had brought along from the cafe, and they went back into the cabin. The boy made a small fire in the old stove and put on a pot of water for coffee. They lit the kerosene lantern, ate cheese and bread and meat, and drank coffee.

"How the hell we going to find out?" Morgan wanted to know.

"There's one Indian from the tribe who works in Lost Canyon. He's read the law. He even makes speeches sometimes. And he's been clear to Washington to see the president. Maybe we can get him to take us to the chief."

"I sure want to talk to that chief," Morgan said. "Can you see this guy when we get back to town in the morning?"

"First thing," Jason promised. "If he's not

gone on some business out of town. He's gettin'
to be a real big shot, even if he is an Indian.
Name's Grey Stoneagle.''

Jason got them some blankets and they
bedded down on the floor. Although they didn't
speak of it, neither of them seemed to want to
sleep on the bed where they had found old
Gramps.

Morgan put his black snake whip and his
gunbelt with the Bisley Colts, along with the
rifle, by his side and lay down. He thought
about the gold for a little while, wondering
about the Indian chief and what good it would
do to see him.

In a little while he began to think about Celia
Fair and wishing she hadn't gone off on the
stage to Salt Lake City, to take the train to
Chicago and Boston. He was feeling horny again
already, and she had been so good.

So beautiful and so good. She'd learned it all
from her Swedish nanny? He didn't like to think
of her wasting it on some other man that she
might meet in Chicago. Or Boston. God, what
ailed him, anyhow. Lee Morgan didn't go
mooning around after some woman he'd had.

She was gone. She'd had her fling and left to
take care of her father's business. He would
probably never see her again, so he had better
forget her and get on with his life and his search
for the gold.

8

Morgan and Jason woke late and had coffee and biscuits, then saddled up for the ride back to town. Before they went, they found some paper and a stub of a pencil with which Morgan made a sketch of the carving he had found on the log at the back corner of the cabin. He studied it for some time after he had drawn it on the paper. He compared it to the symbols carved in the log and decided it was near enough. Then he folded it and put it in the pocket with Hank's money and note.

Why would anyone want to hide gold in a tepee? Would Hex or Gramps, either one, have trusted the old Indian chief that much? After all, the Indians could have used the gold. They might not have had as much know-how about where to have it melted down and put in more exchangeable sizes, the way Hex Downs would have, but Morgan couldn't imagine either himself or Broom trusting an Indian like that— not even a Chief.

Maybe it was just the secret that lay with the chief? Or another clue? They would have to find a way to meet with him to discover whether he had any such information.

While Morgan was making the drawing,

Jason took a broom and whisked at the dirt by the back door, across the trail as it led up to the front door, and anywhere else he thought hoofprints would show up, if someone came to the cabin before he did the next time.

"Good work," Morgan said. "You're a smart kid, Jason."

"Sometimes I have an idea or two," Jason said. "Sure can't figure out why Gramps would leave what we're looking for with the old chief. 'Specially with his son being such an enemy of the whites and next in line to run the tribe. The old chief could die off. . . ." He let that thought fade, apparently thinking again of the fact that his Gramps was gone.

It was afternoon when they finally got back to Lost Canyon. Morgan said, "You're going to get together with this dude Indian that lives in town, huh?"

"I'll find him. I told you, his name is Grey Stoneagle. He lives over the barber shop, I think. I'm sure he used to. Anyhow, the barber will know."

"If you find him soon enough, maybe he'll be able to take us to see the chief by tomorrow. What do you think?"

Jason nodded. "I'll try. Then I'll go to work, so I can get off again tomorrow to go."

"Good. You sure this town Indian gets along okay with the rest of them? That chief's son might recognize me from before."

"He won't do anything about it if we're escorted in," Jason said. "He does things his father doesn't approve of when he's away from the camp. But I don't think he'd defy him, if Grey Stoneagle gets the chief's permission first."

Morgan put his horse in the livery, took his black snake and started out the door.

Sheriff Tyler came stomping down the street and stopped when he saw Morgan. "You still here?"

"Gotta wait around till I get Hank Broom properly put under the ground, Sheriff." Morgan narrowed his eyes at the sheriff, daring him to try to drive him out of town in the face of his obvious concern for a dead friend's burial.

"Likely get that taken care of today, won't you? Awful warm this week. Wouldn't want to wait too long." The sheriff's lip curled into a sneer and he moved on.

The stableman's son, Willie, and his dog, stood at the corner of the building watching. The livery owner remained inside, but Morgan knew he had been within hearing range.

Morgan waited until the lawman was well past, then turned to the boy. "You know an Indian fellow, name of Stoneagle, that keeps a place here in town, Willie?"

"I might," the boy said, eyeing Morgan cagily.

"Just wondered where a person might get in touch with him."

The boy said nothing.

Morgan took a coin from his pocket and flipped it in the air, catching it and flipping it again.

The boy got to his feet. "I see him sometimes."

"Well, I'd like to see him, myself."

Morgan flipped the coin again, this time toward Willie who caught it and smiled broadly. "I'll probably see him."

As Morgan turned to leave, the boy called after him, "Had my druthers, I'd like to learn about that whip of yourn, Mr. Morgan."

"We'll see."

Morgan went down the street to the hotel. He stopped and asked at the desk whether Nelly was filling the tub that afternoon.

"She could do that," Jeb said. "Right away."

"Thanks. I'll get ready."

Morgan noticed a woman sitting in one of the lobby chairs. She wore a dark red dress with long sleeves and buttoned high at the neck. Her hair had been swooped up and pinned high on her head and with the afternoon sun coming in side windows of the lobby it made her look as if she wore a halo. She had sharp features, but was not unattractive. Maybe about Morgan's age, she sat quite still, holding onto her reticule and gazing toward the door. Morgan wondered if she were waiting for someone.

She didn't appear to notice him. Usually a woman would at least look at him, so he could nod or tip his Stetson. He went on up the stairs to his room.

Nelly brought water to the bathtub again. Morgan asked her who the woman sitting in the lobby was.

"Said something about Brant Corson," Nelly said. "But her name's not Corson."

"What is her name?"

"Rebecca Petersen," Nelly told him. "Think you know her from somewhere?"

"No, I don't think so. Yet—"

Morgan took off his shirt and winked at the blushing Nelly who picked up her pails and prepared to leave the room.

"Wait just a minute," Morgan said. After he had arranged for Nelly to get a bit of laundry taken care of for him, he gave her enough to pay for that and a small tip.

"Thank you, Mr. Morgan. I'll see these get done up right away."

She left, and Morgan bathed and dressed. Then he went back downstairs.

The woman still sat in the same position assuming the same attitude.

Morgan went up to her. "Excuse me, Madam. Do you know what time it is?"

She started, then glanced up at him. He eyes were bright blue. She looked younger than he had thought at first. Now that the sun was no longer shining in on it, her hair proved to be pale blonde and still looked like a halo, piled high on her head as it was.

"Oh . . . I . . . Maybe." She fingered a watch hanging on a gold chain around her neck. She stared at it, as if surprised to find it there.

"I think it's supper time," Morgan said. "Are you planning to eat your evening meal with someone?"

She shook her head mournfully. "Not any more."

Morgan sat in the chair next to her. "What do you mean?"

"He's dead."

"Oh. That's too bad."

Rebecca Petersen looked at Morgan, as if seeing him for the first time. "Well, maybe it's too bad. He was too bad, too. Did you know him?"

"Who?" Morgan asked.

She was really quite pretty. If, as Nelly had suggested, she had someting to do with Brant Corson, she had something in common with Morgan. They both were left with someone to forget on this pleasant summer evening, just dipping into night.

"Brant Corson," she said. "Did you know him?" she asked again.

"Only by sight," Morgan told her. "I heard he. . . ."

"He was shot." She was quiet for a moment, then added as an afterthought, "Probably with good reason."

She sighed a deep shaky sigh that sounded as if it came clear from her pointy-toed buttoned shoes. The sigh apparently opened the way for more words. "I came over from Reno. I thought Brant had struck it rich out here. He was going to. Instead, I come and find out he's stone dead. I should have come earlier. Damn Bert Tyler!"

Morgan was sure he wanted to hear more about that last remark. "Come across the street and have some dinner with me," he suggested. "We've both been left on our own in a strange town."

"You're alone, too?"

"My friend left town," Morgan said. He stood and put out a hand to help Rebecca Petersen to her feet.

Rebecca accepted. The top of her head came about to Morgan's nose. Just a nice fit. She was thin of waist and hip, but had an ample bosom, outstanding, in fact.

They went over to the cafe and found a table in the back corner. Morgan held Rebecca's chair, then sat where he could watch everyone who came or went. It hadn't done much good to be able to see Brant Corson when he came in the day before. But he liked to be able to see anyhow.

"Little wine to start out with?" Morgan asked. "Or a beer?"

When the woman had tasted a glass of wine, she seemed to relax a little. "I'm going to head for San Francisco when the next stage comes that's going that way."

"You have kin in San Francisco?"

"My daddy lives there. He was right. I never should have left home in the first place."

"So this Corson who was shot yesterday was your—" He let the sentence dangle.

Rebecca picked it up and finished it. "Man. He was my man. We were together in Reno and did right well, till he got this big idea about coming over here."

"What did you do there?"

"I danced. They had a fancy saloon there with dancing shows. Brant was good at cards and other things."

They were quiet for a stretch during which Florrie came over with the food they had ordered.

"Hope everything is all right," Florrie said, setting down Morgan's plate.

"Everything will be fine," he said. "You always work from morning to night?"

"Pretty much," Florrie didn't sound as if she minded.

"Florrie, this is Rebecca, visiting town from Reno."

The two women acknowledged the introduction.

Morgan asked Florrie, "Jason working this evening?"

"Yes, but he has tomorrow off. Said you might want to know."

"Good."

Florrie left them and Morgan turned his attention to Rebecca Petersen. "How's it going?"

"Fine. I'm feeling better, thanks to you, Mr. Morgan."

"Call me Lee, please."

"All right. If you'll call me. . . ." She hesitated, as if remembering what Corson called her.

"I'll call you Rebecca, if that's all right."

"That's my name. I really don't like nicknames, do you, Lee?"

"Luckily I haven't had to deal with any," he said.

"Corson called me Rebby and I didn't like that," she admitted. "I guess I shouldn't cry about him being gone, or carry on too much. There were a lot of things about Brant Corson I didn't like. But I think Bert Tyler was to blame for all Brant's troubles."

"The sheriff?" Morgan asked, trying to sound surprised.

"We knew him in Reno," Rebecca said. "He wasn't any sheriff then."

When they had finished eating, Morgan asked what she would like to do. "I suppose we could sample some of the great night life in this teeming metropolis of Lost Canyon."

They laughed together. She had a nice laugh, throaty and enduring.

"You're fun . . . Lee." She hesitated before saying his name.

"I like talking to you, too. Maybe we could go somewhere quiet. Find us a bottle and have a little nightcap," Morgan suggested.

Rebecca sat up straighter, raised her eyebrows and appeared to have a brilliant idea. "I have what they call over in Reno, 'an excellent bottle.' It's in my room at the hotel." After hesitating a moment she added, with a smile, "It's brandy. I stole it in Reno before I came here."

Morgan laughed with her again. "That's the best kind." He liked her down-to-earth manner, now that she had relaxed enough to let it out.

He paid the bill, said good night to Florrie, and offered Rebecca his arm as they left the cafe.

They went into the hotel and both picked up their keys at the desk. There was no sense in scandalizing the Rowes by advertising that they were both going to one room.

Rebecca had room twenty-nine down the hall from his, right next door to where he bathed. Actually it was right next door to where everybody on the second floor bathed, the ones who did.

They went in and left the door open while Morgan lighted her kerosene lamp for her. Then Rebecca closed the door and slid the bolt into place. She dug the bottle out of her bureau drawer and to Morgan's surprise brought out two small brandy snifters as well.

Her blue eyes twinkled and she nodded. "Yes. I stole those, too. Thought I was going to do some celebrating."

Morgan opened the bottle for her and poured. "We will do some celebrating. We'll celebrate our new friendship."

She sat on the edge of the bed and Morgan sat beside her.

He ran the brandy glass back and forth under his nose. "Smells darn good to me. Here's to friendship."

She touched her glass to his and sipped. "Ooo. That's warming, isn't it?"

"Smooth," Morgan said, drawling the word

out.

The silence grew for a minute or two and Rebecca took a couple more sips of her brandy, as if trying to relax again. "I guess I'm sort of nervous."

"That's because the friendship we're drinking to is so young," Morgan told her. "Incidentally, how young are you?"

"Didn't your mama ever teach you not to ask a lady's age?" she asked. But she began to smile again.

"I wouldn't want to try to give you a kiss, if it would get me into too much trouble," Morgan kidded, grinning back at her.

"You're kinda good looking," Rebecca said, scanning his features. "I had a friend in Reno who used to say she was old enough to know better."

"But too young to resist?" Morgan shot back.

"I'm nineteen. But I'll be twenty in a day or so."

"Then I guess I'll kiss you before you get too old," he said. He reached across her and set his glass down on the bedside table, took her glass out of her hand and set it beside his.

Her blue eyes gazed into his and a slight smile rested on her lips. He kissed her. A gentle testing kiss. A kiss that a young lady in a strange town wouldn't be able to resist.

She didn't resist.

He kissed her again, still tenderly, but more enduring. She slid her arms around his neck.

He embraced her holding her close and feeling the firm full breasts against his chest. He wanted to feel them next to his bare skin. But he had no idea how much experience she had had. He had no desire to frighten her.

On the other hand, she had said Corson was her *man*. Morgan moved a hand up and down her back, slowly. She responded by pressing her body closer to his and making her lips softer under his kiss.

Lee moved his lips from hers to her neck, just below her ear. Her high-necked dress didn't permit much maneuvering there, so he unbuttoned her top button. In moments they were both rapidly shedding clothing and almost instantly found themselves back on the bed naked.

He reached into her hair to pluck out a pin. She helped him, and the blonde silk cascaded down around her shoulders and back. "It's beautiful," he said.

She smiled and they embraced. He lay her back against the pillows and kissed her. Then he drew away and looked at her.

Her breasts were magnificent. He liked women with small firm breasts too, but this was a treasure trove. He fondled them, nursed them and caressed them. He couldn't leave them alone.

He straddled her and lay his rapidly growing rod between her breasts and squeezed them together against it.

Rebecca did nothing to prevent him. Her blue eyes gazed at him in wonder and the slight vaguely interested smile still played on her lips. He couldn't tell whether she was becoming aroused or not.

He swung his leg back over her and slid down beside her, giving her another kiss on the lips and then running his tongue between her breasts and on down her middle. She giggled.

Teasing her nipples with kisses and nibbles

while sliding his hand down across her flat belly to the furry mound below it, Lee felt the buds on her breasts harden and heard her murmur, "Mmmm."

He moved his main focus of attention to the slit in the furriness and agitated her love button with his fingers. His lips refused to leave the fantastic breasts. But she now became more obviously excited. The more he played, the more her body responded.

She finally put her hand out and touched his leg, then cautiously ran the hand up to find his throbbing organ. She clasped it in her hand and seemed to urge it toward her.

"Roll over," he said.

Lee told hold of her waist and helped her turn over, boosting her buttocks, so that she rested on her knees and elbows, showing her rosebud ass.

He got behind her on his knees and felt for her now moist and swollen hole. He gently slid his rod into the eager cunt, closed the space between them, and leaned over her so his arms went around her and fondled her breasts while he worked in and out of her, doggie style.

Before he got too far to control it, he wanted her ready too, so he moved one hand down the front of her and diddled her most excitable spot some more, while pumping in and out.

She emitted little cries of pleasure and lifted her rump to meet his pushes. Their efforts were at first slow and teasing and then became urgent, strong, and faster until Lee could hold back no longer. As he released his hot juices into her, she called out, "Oh, yes."

Presently they rolled over onto one side. Still

engaged, Lee held her closely in his arms. Cupped like spoons, they lay breathing deep satisfied breaths.

The lamp wick flickered. They paid no attention, letting it die out on its own. Before they fell asleep, Lee heard her sigh and murmur, "I never had it that good."

Sometime during the night, Lee felt Rebecca's silken hair fall across his chest as she turned and snuggled close to him. He put his hand on her breast and felt the nipple harden in his fingers.

His groin awoke and in a moment his rod was hard and ready again. They rejoined, in the dark. This time, he pulled her on top of him, afraid that he might crush her if he mounted her straight away.

He grasped her firm buttocks and rocked her as she leaned forward so that her two great globes touched his face. He took first one then the other by its tip sucking until finally he forgot them in the rush of another release.

Rebecca rested on top of him, her breasts pressing on his chest, her fine hair falling across his arm, her heart beating hard, and her breath again coming in gasps, as was his own.

"Oh, you!" she said. And again they slept.

In the morning, the sun was already beating in through the lace curtains when they woke. Lee opened his eyes to see Rebecca leaning on one elbow looking down at him. Her eyes were just as blue in the daylight as they had been at night. Her long pale hair hung to the side, over the arm she rested on.

"Aren't you a pretty sight to wake up to," Morgan said.

"We could stay right here all day," Rebecca said, then bit her lip, as if she thought she had spoken out of turn.

"That would be almost perfect, except for one or two things," Lee told her. "I have to go and meet someone. And I have to bury a friend today."

Rebecca gasped. "Oh, that's right. I did mine yesterday. Only I don't think his brother wanted me there."

Lee leaned over and kissed the girl, then got out of bed and started putting on his pants. "So what are you going to do?"

"I don't know. I guess I'll have to go and ask Bert Tyler."

Morgan made no comment on Sheriff Bert Tyler. She had known him in Reno, and possibly thought the sheriff would give her some of Corson's things.

"Well, I have to see about my friend that died the same day. His name was Hank Broom." He pulled on his shirt and tucked it in.

"Did your friend get shot too?"

Morgan just nodded. No use telling her that her erstwhile man shot his friend.

"I'll see you later," Morgan said. He smiled down at her. "I liked it too." Maybe it had been simpler, after all, when females ran off in the early hours before you woke, and you didn't have to think what to say or how to get away without making them feel rejected.

He glanced out the door to see who was about, not wanting to compromise the lady. Finding the hall empty he headed for his own room.

He had been inside only a minute or two, when there was a tap on the door. He hoped it wasn't going to be Rebecca getting clingy.

It was a tall Indian dressed in a dark well-cut business suit. His blue-black hair was cut to a modest length, with the back slightly longer than the sides. He removed a well-blocked gray felt hat and asked in cultivated tones, "Mr. Morgan?"

"Yes."

"I'm Grey Stoneagle. Young Willie said you were looking for me."

"Come in." Morgan stood back so Grey Stoneagle could accept the invitation. "Have you seen Jason Isley?"

"Yes. Last night. He told me what you want. But I wished to speak to you, before we go."

Morgan indicated the chair, but Stoneagle shook his head. "I'll be only a minute." He looked Morgan straight in the eyes. "We will go to my old chief in peace."

"Of course." Morgan had never known an Indian who spoke such perfect English, who had manners better than the last U.S. Senator he had known. Then he decided he had better level with this man who was about to help him and Jason with their mission. "We go in peace, but there may be one problem."

Stoneagle stood hat in hand waiting, attention.

"A few days ago, a small group of Washos set on a friend and me as we were on the trail up to Ole Olmanson's cabin. There was an exchange of gun fire."

"I know about it," Stoneagle said. "I have made arrangements. It will be all right. Chief Greatfoot will see you. We will go when you are through with your ceremony. We will meet at the stables." He didn't offer to shake hands, just nodded and left, putting his hat on as he went out into the hall.

Morgan watched Grey Stoneagle until he disappeared down the stairway. He moved like a panther. A panther in a business suit. Silent and smooth. And he knew everything that was going on. He would see Morgan after the ceremony.

Just before noon, the old cemetery, behind the church and partly enclosed in a forged iron fence, accepted the remains of Hank Broom.

A modest gathering of certain townsfolk heard the Reverend intone something about ashes and dust.

Jeb and Essie Rowe were there, having apparently left Nelly to hold the fort back at the hotel.

The barber had closed his shop for an hour and stood by, having done the same the day before for Brant Corson, according to Jason. Morgan couldn't imagine why the barber had attended the earlier service as Corson never looked as if he'd had his hair cut or washed in his entire lifetime. Perhaps going to funerals was a tradition with him.

A couple of highly rouged ladies from Hank's favorite saloon wept prettily into their hankies.

Jason stood next to Morgan and held Florrie's hand. Florrie had brought a little clutch of hand-picked flowers, as had Essie Rowe.

A group of kind and thoughtful people.

The sheriff stood on the periphery of the small assembly and watched. He left without comment as the first spadeful of dirt was returned to the six-foot hole. Morgan wondered if Tyler assumed he would now leave town.

If so, he assumed wrong.

9

Back from the cemetery, Morgan tried to put Broom's death behind him. There was work to be done, work that Hank had started and Morgan intended to finish.

Lee headed for the livery to meet Jason and Stoneagle. The Indian was an enigma, probably the product of some Indian agent who, as an example, sent him off to school to be educated. An example of what? And whose side would Stoneagle take in a fight?

He had promised to lead them to Chief Greatfoot. Jason and Lee would be two white men threading through hostile Indian territory, with only Stoneagle's word that the chief would talk to them in peace. By nightfall they could be two bloody scalps hanging in Greatfoot's camp.

Across the street in the sheriff's office, Morgan glimpsed Rebecca Petersen. He wished he were closer so he could overhear the conversation between Rebecca and Sheriff Tyler. Her gloved hands moved in animated gestures. Did the gestures designate anger or was she simply explaining something to Tyler? Perhaps she wanted to claim Corson's belongings. Maybe she was trying to find out whether her man had struck it rich before he died.

At the livery, Morgan's horse whinnied in recognition when he spoke. Lee patted the horse's shoulder, then ran his hand gently across the animal's soft muzzle. The horse nuzzled Morgan's fingers. "Now what do you want? You've been fed. I know Willie fed you this morning."

Morgan dug into the pocket of his denims and brought out a lump of sugar he'd taken from the cafe at breakfast. "This what you're after?" He held the sugar in his palm and the horse accepted it.

Morgan lifted his saddle from the rack and secured it on the back of his mount, checked the cinch a second time, took the rifle out of the boot and made sure it was loaded. Then he turned to look for Jason and Stoneagle.

The Indian stood silently against the wall. Did Morgan detect a ghost of a smile on Stoneagle's face? Or perhaps it was a sneer. "Jason will be here in a moment," the Indian said. "He is escorting Florrie back to the cafe."

The Indian had changed from his business suit to denims and a brown linen shirt, but he still wore the straight brimmed black hat. Lee noticed that boots, much the same as his own, covered his feet. His gun belt held a Colt forty-five.

Stoneagle disappeared for a moment at the far end of the stable. He returned leading a giant black stallion, complete with saddle and a rifle in the boot. This Indian was either rich or smart. It would take a year's pay to buy a stallion like his, or the cunning of a fox to capture him on the range and break him. Lee had a feeling Stoneagle was smart.

Morgan leaned against the side of the stable. Why did he have misgivings about the Indian? If Jason trusted him, he would have to. There was no other means of getting through the Indian territory to Chief Greatfoot.

In minutes Jason arrived, his eyes bright and a little smug. Florrie must have permitted a kiss when he left her. "Hi, Grey," he greeted the Indian. "Everything all set?"

Stoneagle smiled at Jason. "We are ready to go. The messenger came before daylight. The chief will sit with you and Mr. Morgan."

The three riders headed northwest, in the same general direction as Gramps' cabin.

The sheriff now sat in a chair outside his office fanning himself with a white cardboard, probably a 'wanted' poster. Morgan felt the sheriff's eyes on his back and wondered if he would signal one of his boys to follow them. Rebecca was nowhere in sight. Whatever she had to say to the sheriff evidently was finished.

Out on the trail, Stoneagle led the way. Jason and Morgan rode side by side. "How long have you and Stoneagle known each other?" Morgan asked.

"Ever since I came to live with Gramps. He spent a lot of time at Gramps' place. I think he was kind of an outcast in the tribe."

"You trust him? I mean he won't lead us into an ambush, will he?"

"I'd trust him with my life." The indignation in Jason's voice surprised Morgan.

"You *are* trusting him with your life." He wanted to know more about Stoneagle. "Why was he an outcast?"

"I think his father was the son of a chief from

another band of Indians, who married a woman from Greatfoot's tribe. Stoneagle can't be a chief, but Greatfoot's son, Burning Arrow, has always been afraid he might try to take his place. Burning Arrow is always stirring up trouble with the whites. Thinks he's a warrior."

"It must have been Burning Arrow and his friends who attacked me and Broom the day we found your Gramps."

"He and his bunch of renegade warriors have killed a lot of white people. Some in the town, but mostly they attack wagon trains and supply trains. He hates whites. He kills everybody on the trains."

"Why don't they go after them? Send the army after them?"

Jason grinned. "Wait until you see the entrance to the camp, then you'll know why. Nobody can find it."

The summer sun beat down on Morgan's shoulders. They should have left earlier. The sandy trail they followed was clear of growth, but low desert bushes dotted the ground on either side. Up ahead the cool green of the mountains beckoned, but Stoneagle led them around the base of the mountain.

About two hours into the desert, Stoneagle stopped and dismounted at what appeared to be a tiny oasis. "We must rest the horses. Soon we will climb a steep trail up there." He pointed to a ridge of mountains in the distance. "I am sorry there is no water here at this time of year, but there will be plenty of water at the high spring."

Jason and Morgan got off their horses and sat cross-legged in the shade. Morgan's gaze scanned the countryside for landmarks in case he needed to come here without a guide. He noted a camelback rock on the crest of a hill.

Stoneagle smiled. "Finding Chief Greatfoot's camp would not be a problem for you, but you would never gain entrance without a guide, one already expected by the chief."

"Well guarded?"

"Even without the guards, you would not get in."

Morgan didn't pursue the subject. He had heard about Indian camps with entrances that were impossible to find. About beautiful fertile valleys surrounded by tall mountains loaded with game, deer and wild turkeys for food.

A few miles later, the upward climb began. With no trail visible, Stoneagle led the way. No wonder the white man often got ambushed. He always went the same way and wore a trail. Evidently Greatfoot's tribe never took the same path twice.

Up and up they climbed. Stoneagle led them back and forth like a million hairpins hooked together. Morgan and Jason dismounted and led their horses. Only a trained mountain horse could scale these rocks with a rider, without danger of falling. Stoneagle's stallion had no trouble.

At the spring, they stopped to water the horses and to eat the lunch Florrie had packed. Cheese and biscuits and strips of beef. The Indian appeared to savor their food. He had truly become a white man in everything but the color of his skin.

"Stoneagle, I assume you will interpret for us?"

"If needed. The chief speaks English. If he knows where the gold is hidden he will tell you.

It is of no value to him."

Morgan didn't mask his surprise. "So you
know about the gold, too?"

"I would not have brought you here without
knowing why you wanted to come." Stoneagle
got to his feet. "We must go. The entrance to the
camp is near by."

The Indian didn't mount his stallion, but led
it along behind him. They must have gone a
hundred yards, when suddenly out of nowhere,
they were completely surrounded by Indian
braves. One addressed Stoneagle angrily. "So
the white Indian who is a coward has brought
white murderers to our camp. I order you to
take them away."

No one had to tell Morgan this young brave
was Burning Arrow, the son of the chief. He'd
seldom seen such hate on a man's face.

"You do not order me, Burning Arrow, I have
a message of safe passage from the chief, your
father, for these two men."

A half dozen braves stood their ground.
Morgan's gaze scanned the long rock formation
in front of them. They might be going in, but
where?

Stoneagle advanced along the rock face.
"Stay close behind me."

Burning Arrow jumped into Stoneagle's path.
He raised his war ax. "One more step and I will
kill you."

Morgan wondered at the force of the anger on
the young Indian's face. No emotion at all
showed on Stoneagle's. With a swift movement
he reached forward and wrested the war ax
from Burning Arrow. "You will step back and
permit us to enter."

"I will kill you," Burning Arrow rasped

between clenched teeth, but he moved away and the three of them went on.

For several more yards, Morgan and Jason followed Stoneagle along the rocky wall. Suddenly the Indian disappeared. The two men stood alone. Jason scowled, ran his hand along the wall.

A bush moved and Stoneagle reappeared, his eyes dancing with amusement. "Thought you two were following me."

"We were, but—" Jason began. Then he grinned at his own stupidity. Jason and Morgan stepped around the bush and following Stoneagle, threaded their way back and forth through a maze of rock corridors.

When they passed the last rock into the trees, the fresh aroma of pine filled the air. They led their horses fifty yards or so down the tree covered hillside and stopped. Below, a long green valley stretched for maybe five miles. In the middle of the valley, at least fifty neat tepees formed a colorful circle.

Morgan whistled under his breath. Green mountains completely surrounded the Indian camp, giving adequate water to the lush grazing land.

Morgan heard a rustle behind him in the trees. His hand automatically reached for his Bisley. Had Burning Arrow and his braves come in and planned to trap them inside?"

"Put your gun away," Stoneagle said. "You have been granted safe passage. No one will attack you inside the camp. Not even Burning Arrow."

Morgan could almost taste the hostility of Burning Arrow as he and his men trailed behind them to the brightly decorated tepee at the center of the camp.

In front of the tepee, the chief, a grizzled man, near the age of Gramps, sat cross-legged on a buffalo robe. "Son of my gray-haired blood brother, please sit."

Jason sat down.

The chief indicated Morgan. "Is this your friend who wishes to speak?"

"This is my friend, Lee Morgan," Jason said.

Morgan and Stoneagle were invited to sit, and did.

"Jason's Gramps knew about some stolen gold bars. The man who stole them is dead. We want to find the bars. Did Gramps give them to you, or tell you where they were hidden?"

"We want to return them to their rightful owner, Chief Greatfoot," Jason said.

Morgan was having second thoughts about Jason. Did he really plan to return the gold to the railroad for the reward, or was he using a ploy to get the information? No, Morgan was sure Jason meant to return the gold.

The old chief sat thoughtfully for several minutes. "My blood brother spoke of the gold that his friend had brought to the village, but he did not give it to me. He told me he would tell his friend to hide it in a safe place."

"Did he say where he planned to tell his friend to hide it? Give you a message that might indicate the hiding place?"

"No. My blood brother would not endanger my people by giving me such a message."

Morgan sensed Burning Arrow's presence behind him, but tried to ignore the uneasiness it caused. He got to his feet. "I thank you for letting me speak, and for granting me safe passage into your camp. We must not keep you longer."

The old Indian nodded, but said nothing. Morgan and Jason, following Stoneagle's example, mounted their horses and headed for the exit from the camp.

When they were some distance away, Jason leaned toward Lee. "Did you believe him?"

"Yes. I think he's a truthful man. He could buy guns with the gold. Why did Stoneagle say it was of no use to him?"

Stoneagle rode up beside them. "The chief does not want guns, but Burning Arrow does. If he could find the gold, he would buy guns. The chief is old and losing his power. If Burning Arrow takes over the tribe, or even a part of it, you may be sure that many white men will die."

Morgan glanced around for the young would-be chief. He was nowhere in sight. Uneasily, Lee followed Stoneagle and Jason through the labyrinth of rocks out of the camp. He didn't trust Burning Arrow, or his young braves, especially in this timbered area where their horses would be accustomed to navigating the steep terrain.

"Let's get out of these trees," Morgan said. But he was too late. An arrow found its mark. Stoneagle slumped forward on his stallion, an arrow protruding from his shoulder. An Indian had shot Stoneagle in the back.

The stallion kept going, carrying Stoneagle down the mountain. In one quick fluid motion, Morgan and Jason abandoned their mounts and scrambled behind rocks. Their horses followed the stallion.

Jason glanced at Morgan beside him. "Good,

you got your rifle."

"Watch your back," Morgan warned.

Jason watched. Suddenly his Colt forty-five barked and a young brave toppled from an overhanging precipice, falling face down practically at their feet. Blood spurted from his neck, blood and flesh had been spread across his shoulders, and the blood pulsed down his bare, coppery back.

"How many more?" Morgan whispered.

"Don't know."

"Over there." Morgan aimed his rifle. The shot missed. Two arrows glanced off the rock, inches from Morgan's head. "There's at least two more." He sensed the braves creeping closer. He couldn't see them or hear them, but he knew they were closing in.

He nudged Jason and pointed to where a leaf moved, but only one. Their vulnerable position made them an easy target if the Indians got behind them, but nothing nearby offered anything better. Morgan watched the leaves in that spot for several seconds.

One moved again. He fired, once, twice.

No arrow returned his fire. The branch the leaves hung on moved, swayed, and bent nearly to the ground. An Indian brave pitched forward. He lay motionless on the ground, his back blown open by Morgan's shot.

"You got him." Jason got halfway to his feet.

Morgan jerked him back to the ground. An arrow whizzed by where Jason had been. "There's at least one more."

Jason appeared shaken. "Let's get out of here."

"How? Burning Arrow is still out there. If we

make a run for it, he'll get one of us for sure. Just wait, he'll make his move."

They waited. Ten minutes passed, then twenty. Morgan's nerves threatened to explode. He could see that Jason's were no better. An old Indian trick. Wait. Wait until the opponent could no longer stand the strain and left his cover. Well, Lee and Jason wouldn't bite.

They stayed put behind their rocks, not moving, not talking, just watching in every direction. Finally Morgan edged a few feet to the left, motioned Jason to do likewise.

A sudden movement, not ten yards away, jarred their nerves. Jason raised his Colt. Morgan shook his head. "Decoy." He had fought hostile Indians more than once, and throwing an object, a rock or a limb, to get an enemy's attention, was an old trick. It gave the Indian a chance to reposition.

Several more minutes passed. An arrow from behind missed Morgan's head by inches and glanced off the rock.

Morgan spun around, fired several rounds into the trees. A noisy thrashing in the brush answered, then hooves pounded the ground. Morgan rose slowly from his crouched position and peered over the rocks. A horse, carrying a rider with blood trailing a thin line down the back of his bare arm, galloped toward the Indian camp.

"You got Burning Arrow," Jason said. "He wears that headband with the colors of the chief."

He's barely wounded. See how well he sits his horse?"

Jason holstered his gun. "Well, at least he's

going home. Think there are any others?"

Near the edge of the timber line, they could see three riderless horses drinking at the spring. Both men broke into a run, jumping from rock to rock and over tree roots that threatened to throw them headlong down the mountain.

Stoneagle lay beside the spring breathing raggedly. "Arrow. Bleeding," he gasped.

An arrow protruded from deep in his shoulder. Morgan stripped part of the Indian's shirt away. "Can't take it out, you'll bleed to death." He broke off a stick half an inch in diameter, and placed it between Stoneagle's teeth. "Bite down hard, I've got to break off the arrow's shaft."

Drops of perspiration wet Morgan's brow as he positioned the sturdy arrow between his closed fists. He gathered his strength, then in one quick motion bent the shaft. It snapped. He wadded up the torn shirt and wrapped the wound and the broken end of the arrow, then tied it in place. "You've got to travel now to get to the doctor."

Stoneagle nodded. Jason and Morgan lifted him onto his horse. Morgan took the reins and mounted the stallion, sitting behind Stoneagle. "We've got to move fast," he said to Jason. "Tie my horse behind yours and let's go."

The eight or ten miles ahead, under the desert sun, didn't look promising for Stoneagle. He'd lost a lot of blood, and the jarring ride could cause him to lose more.

For the first hour they moved along at a good gait. By grasping Stoneagle around the middle, Morgan could hold him in a somewhat upright position, but twice he accidentally bumped the broken shaft of the arrow, and the Indian had gasped in pain.

They stopped to rest the horses. Although the stallion was a mighty horse, carrying two riders in the afternoon sun could throw him lame. He thought of walking and leading the stallion, but Stoneagle could not sit his horse alone.

The next few miles of the trip became more difficult. Stoneagle could no longer raise his head to drink from the canteen. Morgan wet a piece of his shirt tail and laid it across the back of the Indian's neck. At intervals, he soaked it from the canteen.

They could see the shadows of Lost Canyon in the distance when Stoneagle, now unconscious, slumped forward against the neck of his horse. Morgan could no longer hold him in even a semi-sitting position. By now blood soaked the compress and the back of what was left of the Indian's shirt. Soon he could die.

They still had a couple of miles to go when Morgan signaled to Jason. "Ride on ahead and make sure the doc is ready for us."

"I'll find him and tell him you're coming in," Jason promised, and galloped into town.

Morgan poured the last of the water over Stoneagle's head. "We're almost home," he said.

Stoneagle moved slightly but didn't answer. At least he was still alive.

Morgan urged the stallion to go faster. All of Morgan's mistrust of the Indian had disappeared. He wanted Stoneagle to live.

When they came into town, Jason ran to meet them. He took the reins and led the horse to the steps leading to the doctor's house where he had his office. A couple of bystanders helped

Morgan and Jason carry Stoneagle up the steps.

The doctor took over and Morgan waited. If he'd had any sense he would have left the way Jason did, and had Florrie make him something to eat, but he waited until Doc removed the arrow and announced that Stoneagle would live. "Barring infection," he said. "Now Indians are shooting Indians, and in the back yet!" Doc shook his head in disbelief." He decided to keep Stoneagle there. "My wife and daughter will help tend him."

Stoneagle had regained consciousness. He signaled Morgan to his bedside. Pain etched his face, but he spoke clearly. "Do you know if Burning Arrow was killed?"

"I winged him, but he rode off after his braves were dead."

"Be careful, my friend," Stoneagle warned. "Unless the old chief can control them, this could bring many braves from the tribe down on the town."

10

Satisfied that Grey Stoneagle's condition had been attended to the best of the doctor's ability, that he would have someone on hand to care for him, and that there was nothing more he could do, Morgan left.

Jason had already hurried off to his room behind the cafe to get ready to go to work.

Morgan saw to stabling his horse and Stoneagle's and with his trusty black snake whip in hand walked back to the hotel. He picked up his key from Essie Rowe behind the desk and went on up to his room.

Throwing the bolt, he tossed his hat and his whip on the bed. This area was getting downright tiresome with that damn Indian brave coming down on him every time he turned around. And when Burning Arrow wasn't attacking him, it was someone else.

If it weren't for the gold, Morgan thought, he would leave right now. Maybe the gold wasn't worth it anyhow. Maybe he'd best just cut his losses, pack up, and take off. Say to hell with it.

He stomped over to the wash basin, poured in some water from the pitcher and washed his face. He felt agitated and restless.

As he finished toweling his face and head, he

noticed a small scrap of paper lying in the middle of the floor. He hung the towel on the peg and ran a comb through his hair, then picked up the slightly crumpled paper.

Straightening it out, he swore as he saw the hastily scrawled message: *Help me Celia*

Celia! His heart raced. She needed help. But where?

My God! What could this mean? Was Celia still in Lost Canyon? In trouble? Corson was dead. Who could be threatening her now? The men who worked with Corson to find the gold? The men who had killed old Gramps? The men who had chased him and Jason to the caves?

Morgan clapped his Stetson onto his head. He was ready to rush out the door. He'd go to that damn Corson Ranch and see just what the hell was going on. The last man to give Celia trouble had been Brant Corson. Now who else could it be but his brother? He'd go out there and show those bastards. He would kill every one of them if he had to.

He had his hand on the door knob, when he realized that he was about to go off half-cocked. He had always derided Hank Broom for doing that very thing. Jumping in before he was ready. He had to stop and think about this. How had the message reached him? Where had it come from? He went back and sat heavily on the bed and stared at the paper in his hand. Someone put it there. So someone must know.

Why would a call for help come like this? If she were still here in Lost Canyon, why didn't she come to him herself? Unless she couldn't. Somebody had her. But where?

Finally he got up and went down to the lobby. "Mrs. Rowe, I have a problem. Do you know who left this message for me?"

Essie Rowe looked startled. "What? Message? No I don't think we have any messages for you." Obviously flustered, she turned to search the boxes behind the counter. "No messages, Mr. Morgan."

"No, you misunderstood. I already have the message. I wondered how it got in my room." Morgan could swear the woman was trembling. He wondered briefly what was the matter with her.

Nelly came into the lobby from the hall leading to the rooms on the ground floor. "Room six is ready for occupancy now, Essie."

Room six had been Hank Broom's room.

"Oh, I'm sorry," Nelly said, apparently realizing for the first time that Morgan stood there.

"Nelly, will you take over the desk, please. Jeb wants me." With a murmured 'excuse me' Essie Rowe rushed out of the area.

"Have you been helped, Mr. Morgan?"

He frowned after Essie Rowe. "Wonder what's the matter with her?"

Nelly shook her head and shrugged. "Seems all right to me. Just been pretty busy lately."

He laid his key on the desk. "Nelly, did you see someone shoving a piece of paper under my door while I was away?"

"No. I haven't seen anyone near your door." She looked worried. "Did someone tear up your room again?"

"No. Nothing like that. Someone must have put a message under my door."

She told him she didn't know who it could have been.

Morgan headed for the cafe. This thing had

him rattled. He knew he wasn't thinking straight, maybe young Jason could come up with an idea. He strode on through to the kitchen without acknowledging Florrie's greeting.

When he heard what had happened and saw the piece of paper, Jason shook his head. "I thought she'd gone east."

"I thought so too, but why would a message like this be shoved under my door at the hotel? Who would know something about it?"

"Whoever put it there," Jason said. "The folks at the hotel don't know?"

"If somebody over there knows, they haven't said so."

Florrie came into the kitchen. "What's the matter?"

Morgan showed her the paper, too. He would show everyone in town, if necessary.

"Maybe the old woman where Miss Celia lived would know something," Florrie suggested, after thinking for a minute. "Mrs. Smith would be sure to know if Miss Celia is still in town."

"Where? What woman?"

"Mrs. Smith's Ladies Residence," Florrie told him. "Go one street back." She pointed. "Off Main Street. It's the big grayish house with the gingerbread."

"Gingerbread?"

"You know, the fancy scrolls and stuff. Decorations. Has a round room that looks like a tower, except it isn't up high."

Jason said, "Turn to your left at the barber shop and go up the path, it's practically the first house you see. The biggest."

Morgan hadn't done any exploring in the rest

of the town. He had scarcely found time to notice anything but the hotel, livery stable, cafe, and of course the trails out of town to the cabin, the rock quarry, and the Washos' camp. He followed Jason's instructions and found the Victorian house surrounded by big old trees and an expanse of lawn. There were wicker chairs on the veranda.

A small tidy plaque beside the door was engraved,   MRS.   SMITH'S   LADIES RESIDENCE. He twisted the bell handle and heard it sound a metalic clatter on the other side.

A tiny gray-haired lady answered the door. She looked him up and down and inquired in a quavery voice, "Yes, sir? Are you selling something? Or did you come to call on one of my young ladies?"

Morgan removed his hat. "Name's Lee Morgan, ma'am. I wanted to ask about one of your roomers. A Miss Celia Fair."

"I don't call them roomers. They're guests."

"Yes, ma'am. Guests."

"But Miss Fair hasn't been here since, I believe, Tuesday."

Of course it was Tuesday, Morgan thought. She left here Tuesday and stayed all night with him before she got on the stage Wednesday morning.

"She has gone back home in the east. You're too late." The elderly woman looked him up and down again. "Shame, too."

Had he been less concerned, he would have smiled at the implied compliment. "She hasn't been back?"

"You don't get home and back that fast, young man. She's likely got about to Salt Lake

City by now."

Morgan held out the scrap of paper. "I found this piece of paper shoved under my door today."

"Oh, my." Mrs. Smith clutched a fragile almost transparent hand to her heart. "Oh, dear. I do hope it doesn't really mean it."

"I'm trying to find out anything I can about it." Morgan took back the paper and put it in his pocket.

"I think you should call on the sheriff," Mrs. Smith offered.

"I'd even do that if I thought it would help," Morgan muttered, replacing his Stetson and turning to go.

Would he do that? Yes, by God, he would. If that no-good lazy bastard could ever be forced to do his duty, this had to be the time.

In spite of a morbid feeling in the pit of his stomach and doubts of many kinds assailing his brain, Morgan went to the sheriff's office.

"What the hell are you hanging around for now?" Tyler wanted to know. He sat tipped back in his chair with his feet on his desk. The place smelled of cigar smoke.

"Not for any love of the place," Morgan growled. "But something has come up." He took the folded note out of his pocket and showed it. "I need to know what you think of this?"

"Thought you already helped the lady. First thing you did when you got to town, wasn't it?" The sheriff didn't change his position. He tossed the note down on the desk. "It's likely been blowing around the streets since before she left. Somebody probably picked it up long after its need was met."

"Seems to me it could be something else," Morgan said. "Maybe she didn't go on that stagecoach after all."

"Well, now, I would have heard about it, if there'd have been any trouble, like the last time she started to leave." He made an offensive sound halfway between a snort and a laugh. "Corson was the one who was preventin' her. He's dead."

Morgan couldn't trust himself to speak. He snatched up the paper and left the office.

"You better be leavin' too, Morgan," Bert Tyler barked after him. "I've warned you before."

Morgan stopped at the livery stable. "Willie around?"

Willie's pa shrugged. "Out back, I guess. What you want with him?"

"Just wanted to ask him something." The thought crossed Morgan's mind that the stables smelled a lot better than the sheriff's office.

"Ask him what?"

"He does errands or carries messages for people sometimes, doesn't he?"

The stable man shrugged. "Now and again. You got a message you want carried?"

"Just wanted to ask him something," Morgan repeated and made his way around the corner of the building.

When he found Willie he found out nothing, except that Willie still wanted to learn to handle a black snake whip, and that was not news. "Good luck," Willie said.

Discouraged and frustrated, Morgan headed back to the cafe. He went in and sat at the counter.

"Coffee, Mr. Morgan?" Florrie asked.

"I don't know."

"You haven't found out anything?" She set a cup of coffee in front of him. "You better have something to eat. You haven't been in here for a good meal all day. Taking your business elsewhere?"

"No. Haven't felt like eating." Morgan's gut feeling told him that the sheriff was all wrong. This note had been written recently and sent specifically to him. It meant that Celia Fair needed help. He had to find out how he could help her.

"I bet you could think better if you just had a nice plate of stew," Florrie insisted. "And I'll tell Jason you're here."

Celia heard them coming back. They kept her tied up most all of the time now. She never should have tried to get out the window. Now she would never have another chance. They tied and gagged her every time they left the room. And sometimes they were gone for so long she could hardly stand it.

She kept trying to keep her hopes up, that her message had reached Lee Morgan. But she hadn't been able to put enough in the note. He wouldn't even know where she was, if he got it. She didn't even know where she was. She was sure it was the hotel, but she didn't know which room. No one ever came to clean up. She wondered if the hotel people were in on this too. No. Not Essie Rowe. She was such a nice person. But didn't the hotel owners wonder what was going on in here?

The last time the men came back, they brought bread and cheese and cold coffee. The one called Axel had his arm in a sling. Celia wondered what had happened to him, but when she asked, the bossy one told her to shut her mouth.

This time, the two of them came in and after his usual warning about what would happen to her if she made a sound, the bossy one took the gag out of her mouth. But to her surprise he didn't start asking her things about her brother this time, and he didn't rant about her having stuck him with the wrong bag when she got off the stage. Instead, he tied the handkerchief around her eyes. What didn't they want her to see?

"Someone's here to talk to you," he said gruffly. "And if you know what's good for you, you'll tell him what he wants to know. He's a lot tougher than old Axel and me."

She heard the door open and close again. She assumed someone else must have come in, someone that she was not supposed to see. Did that mean she would know him, if she saw him?

"Well, now, Miss Highfalutin' Fair," a new voice snarled. "I want you to tell me what you did with the leather bag that Brant Corson wanted from you."

She said nothing. She didn't even realize for a moment that he was waiting for her to speak, she had been listening to his voice so closely. She had heard that voice before, but she couldn't place it.

He kicked at her foot, and said, "Bitch. Answer." It hurt her ankle where it was tied to the chair. She cried out. "Ow! What do you want from me?"

"Just told you. Want to know where that bag is. What was in it? It was the gold wasn't it?"

"What gold? There's no gold in it. Just some

jewelry that belongs to my family."

Why were they treating her like this? They could have the jewelry, if they wanted it. If only they would let her go. But she knew that wasn't what they wanted.

They must want the note that Hex had written her and left with the old man up the trail on the side of the mountain. The note didn't mean anything to her, but it probably would to them. It must have something to do with this gold they were ranting about.

"Now we know that's not what was in the bag." His threatening voice grated on her ears. "It's going to go hard on you, if you don't tell me where it is."

"It's probably in Salt Lake City by now, or maybe on it's way to Boston." There, let them know where it was. What were they going to do with the information? If they found the bag, would they let her go or kill her? How long would it take someone to get clear to Salt Lake City to try to get the bag? Would she have to be tied up all that time, before they decided to kill her?

The men withdrew to the other side of the room. She could hear them mumbling.

Celia decided it was time to do something. How could she hurt more than she already did? She screamed.

One of the men stormed back across the room at her and clouted her a blow across the face so hard that it tipped the chair over. Now she hurt worse. She thought the arm she landed on, between the chair and the floor, must be broken. And her head had hit the floor. The pain was excruciating. She began to sob. She couldn't help it. Now she was in worse shape than before. Nobody had heard the scream apparently. Nobody came pounding on the door.

The handkerchief had slipped from her eyes, but she couldn't see anything. Her back was to the men.

She heard the third man's voice say, "Stupid ass. Now look what you've done. I'm getting out of here." The door opened and closed.

What would they do with her now? She couldn't even think about it. The pain was so great it crowded everything out of her mind. The pain was making her mind go blank. Maybe she would die of it.

After eating his stew, with Florrie urging hot bread with butter melting on it and a cup of coffee as well, Morgan returned to the hotel. He saw Sheriff Tyler on the way. The man obviously was too angry to speak to anyone, even to tell them to leave town.

Morgan sat down in the lobby of the hotel. What would he try next that would butt up to a dead end? Nobody could, or would, tell him anything. Should he go out to the Corson ranch and ask them? If they shot him on sight, it wouldn't help Celia would it? And he still wouldn't know. He'd be dead.

He glanced up at the desk and saw that Essie Rowe was back in her place. He thought about how she had run off so fast when he tried to ask her about the message. Why had she been so frightened? Did it have something to do with what he had asked her?

He stood and as he took his first step toward her, she retreated and disappeared again into the back room. He rang the bell on the desk.

In a moment, Jeb came out from the office in the back. "Yes, sir, Mr. Morgan?"

"Oh, never mind, I'll just pick up my key," Morgan said.

"Is there anything wrong?" Jeb wanted to know. "Had any more trouble with people invading your room?"

Morgan thought about that question for a moment and suddenly realized that someone must have been inside his room, otherwise how did that little piece of paper get to the middle of the floor.

Why hadn't he thought of that before? When you shove a letter under the door of a room, it goes only under the door, until you can't push the last edge of it any further.

"Mr. Morgan? You all right?"

"Not quite, Mr. Rowe." Morgan spoke slowly. "Can we have a word in your office?"

Just then Jason Isley came into the hotel lobby.

Morgan motioned for him to come with them as Rowe led the way to the back.

When they entered the office, Essie quickly got up to go back out to the desk. "I'll just take care of things," she began.

"I'd like to speak to you, too, Mrs. Rowe," Morgan said.

Essie looked positively terrified. "But there's no one on the desk."

"They can ring the bell," Morgan suggested.

"Essie, what's wrong?" her husband wanted to know.

She sat back down without saying anything, twisting the handkerchief she held in her hands.

Morgan got out the piece of paper once again. "I found this in my room." He handed it to Jeb

Rowe. "I believe your wife may be able to tell us how it came to be there."

Rowe studied the paper, frowning. "Essie?"

"Anyone could have put it under your door," Essie said, swallowing hard.

"If someone had put it under the door, I wouldn't have found it in the middle of the room."

"It could have blown to the middle of the room, when you opened the door." The woman was grasping at straws, trying to save herself from what? Who did she think was going to hurt her? Who had given her the note to put in there? The note was from Celia, and Celia certainly wouldn't scare anyone.

"Essie, what do you know about this?" her husband asked.

"What are you afraid of?" Morgan added. "Just tell me where you got the paper in the first place. Celia is in trouble, and I want to know how to help her." Damn the woman. She knew! She was the first person in the whole town that showed the slightest sign that she knew something.

Essie began to weep. "It was in their towels. I didn't know what to do with it. I didn't know what it might mean."

Jason who had been standing quietly just inside the closed door the whole time, finally spoke. "You probably did the right thing with it."

"Whose towels? Where did you get it? Where is she?" Morgan stood, almost shouting.

Jeb Rowe made a move toward him. "There's no call to get riled up. If someone is threatening my wife, I want to know why."

Morgan sat back down, trying to contain his

impatience and his fury. If he didn't find out in time to help Celia, he would strangle both of them.

"The people in that room don't ever want anyone to go in there to clean or anything." Essie's words came haltingly at first. "They made that clear. The man with the trunk. And they just throw the towels in a heap out in the hall when they want clean ones and we put a new pile by the door. Sometimes they take food in and set the tray outside the door when they're through."

"What door?"

"The towels were out there last night and when I took them to be laundered, that's when the piece of paper fell out."

On their feet, Morgan and Jason both spoke at once. "Which room?"

"Number eleven."

Jeb Rowe followed the other two men down the hall. "Now let's go at this thing right," he urged.

"You got a key?" Morgan demanded. "Or do we crash through it?"

"Wait a minute." Rowe stood close to the door and listened. "Sounds like somebody cryin' in there." He knocked.

A man's voice growled, "Who is it?"

"It's your hotel owner," Rowe said. "Got your fresh towels here."

"We already got fresh towels," the voice said. "We're okay."

Jeb put the skeleton key in the lock and turned it. The bolt was thrown, however, so the door wouldn't open. Morgan, with his Bisley Colts in his hand, ran at the door and crashed through. The other men followed close behind him.

Essie Rowe screamed from a little way down the hall. Shots rang out. Morgan saw the woman tied to the chair and lying on her side on the floor. He knew who it was. He shot the nearest man point blank. Blood gushed from the front of his throat, and the man went down before he could finish drawing his weapon. He would never draw another weapon, or another breath.

Morgan pulled a table over onto its side and ducked behind it as the other man fired several shots. Jason Isley fell to the floor.

"Drop that piece or you're a dead man," Morgan advised, leveling over the edge of the upset table at the man's head.

Apparently seeing his friend lying dead on the floor and having no available cover himself convinced Axel that he should end the battle there. "Shit." He threw the forty-five out into the middle of the room. "I've got shot up enough already for these stupid bastards." He raised his one good arm into the air.

Jeb Rowe picked up the gun from the floor and held it on the surrendering man.

Morgan went to the woman on the floor. It was Celia. He said nothing, just drew his knife from his right boot and cut her bonds. Then he turned her carefully, relieving her of the chair.

"Oh, Lee, you found me."

That was all she could say. The pain obviously caused her to faint. She looked like a wilted flower whose fragrance had faded to almost nothing.

Morgan picked her up and lay her gently on the bed. Celia came to and cried out as he felt the injured arm to see if it was broken. Then more tears came.

"You'll be all right," Morgan said soothingly. "You're safe now."

Essie Rowe, who had come running up to the door, cried, "Jeb, are you hurt?"

"Jason," Morgan asked, finally. "You hit bad?"

Jason slowly got to his feet. "Naw. It's just a scratch." His face was the color of the white lace curtains.

"I'll hold this fellow, Mr. Rowe," Morgan said. "Can you get the doc? He was in his office this afternoon."

"Think he had to go out of town. But the barber is pretty good. I'll get him."

The barber came with his first aid kit and checked Celia carefully. "Don't think the arm's broken, but it is bruised real bad. And you've got a nasty bump on the head. Might get a cloth wrung with cold water, Miss Essie."

Essie, having made sure her husband was unhurt, hurried to get spring water and a cloth.

When Jason's scratch, which included a sizeable chunk taken out of his denims and his thigh, had been treated with carbolic and bandaged, the barber pronounced them damn lucky.

Morgan sat on the edge of the bed beside Celia holding her hand.

Axel finally spoke up, pointing to his partner. "What you going to do with him?"

"You sit right there and shut up," Morgan told him. "Or I'll do the same to you as I've already done to him."

Sheriff Tyler, apparently alerted by someone hearing the shots, appeared in the doorway.

"Morgan, I ought to shoot you on sight. You're sittin' here with another dead man on the floor."

"No!" Celia cried. Morgan felt her tense and recognized terror in her voice.

"He's not going to shoot anybody," Morgan told her.

Jeb Rowe said, "This man here and the one on the floor are kidnappers, Sheriff. Held this young woman against her will, right here in my hotel."

"Why didn't you complain earlier?"

"Because I didn't know it. They toted her in here in that trunk over there, unbeknownst to us."

"How can you be sure?" The sheriff gave one of his snorts. "Maybe she was just paying these men a visit."

Celia started to protest. Morgan fumed but held his temper and soothed Celia.

"When you get up and around, Miss, you come down and make your complaint. I'll be in my office until time for the Friday night dance."

Morgan noticed that the sheriff was dressed up, wearing a string tie, a clean shirt and pants, newly polished boots and a snappy looking buckskin jacket.

Morgan fingered the thin strip of leather in his pocket and tried to see whether the sheriff was missing a strand of fringe. He wasn't close enough to tell, but it wouldn't have surprised Morgan to find out that Bert Tyler had been present when an old man was beaten to death in his cabin.

When Tyler had taken Axel away with him and promised to notify the undertaker, Celia clutched at Morgan's arm. "It was him. That was his voice! I'm not going to his office for anything."

"His voice?" Lee wanted to know.

"He was in with them. He was here when they blindfolded me. I was sure I'd heard the voice before."

"Stands to reason," Morgan said.

When she felt steadier, Celia cried, "I've got to get cleaned up. I can't stand it any longer."

Morgan carried her and her carpetbag up the stairs to the dressing room where Nelly filled the tub and offered to play lady's maid.

Before he set her down, Celia gave him a faint smile and a glint of the familiar twinkle momentarily came to her eyes. She whispered into his ear, "If I weren't so beaten up, I'd invite you in."

"I'll be right outside the door. You let Nelly help you this time."

He had no intention of leaving Celia Fair alone for a minute until he knew everything there was to know.

When she had finished her bath, she came out dressed in a long blue nightgown of the finest flannel. Her auburn hair was still damp. It hung around her shoulders and tight little curls framed her face.

He insisted Celia be put to bed in his room. "I'm going to guard her until we can get some outside help. The sheriff is not to be trusted."

Essie had a tray brought, and Celia managed to eat a little while Morgan wolfed down his share. Now that she was safe, his appetite had returned.

When they were alone, Morgan finally asked, "What did they want?"

"The leather bag."

"We have to get the whole story, Celia. These people aren't going to give up just because a couple of them are dead."

"I don't even know the whole story," Celia said. "I told you about coming here to help my brother. Now it sounds as if there was some gold involved." She lay back against the pillows and sighed. "From what has been said, I believe that my brother, Hex, stole the gold."

"That seems about right," Morgan said. "How come your brother's name was Downs?"

"He changed his name when he left home. Father wanted him to take over the family business." Celia looked as if she were going to cry again. "If Father had just let Hex be himself, just stay home and write his poetry, everything would have been all right. But Father didn't think that was manly."

"More manly to rob stages, I guess," Morgan said.

"So he went away and changed his name and got himself killed."

"What about the old man up the mountain? Gramps."

"I got a message and went to see him. He gave me a note from Hex." Celia stopped and wiped her eyes. "I don't even know what it means."

Morgan could almost feel the weight of the gold in his hands. He wiped one of his palms against his pant leg. "What did the note say?"

"It was like his poetry. It said:

Open so to see,
the book lies on the table.
Underneath them all
is the treasure of my fable.

Celia went to sleep in his arms. Morgan held her and thought of the things she had told him. An open book and a table? Underneath a book and a table? There hadn't been any books or tables in old Gramps' clue. There hadn't been any books or tables in Chief Greatfoot's tepee. Morgan couldn't make it add up.

He dozed and dreamed of books and tables. He dreamed of the books at Gramps' cabin and the hand hewn table. He dreamed of his father's library table at Spade Bit back in Idaho where the deed to the ranch was kept in the table drawer.

But in each place, in his dreams, on every table, every book he opened revealed only pictures of men with long stringy hair coming out of tepees and drawing down on him faster than he could reach for his Bisley Colts.

He woke with a start, wondering where he was and why his arm was asleep. The moon shone through the lace curtained windows lighting the room so that he could see Celia's face. He carefully withdrew his arm from underneath her. She stirred but didn't waken.

He still couldn't make any sense of the four-line poem Hex Downs had left his sister. She must have remembered it right. She even wrote it down so he could see how it had looked. It looked like a poem and it rhymed. But that was all he could say for it. What could it have to do with a rainbow and a tepee?

In the morning, when Morgan was up and dressed, he waited for Celia to waken. He wondered if she would still be here or where she would be when she got well enough to want to play again. He switched that train of thought off immediately. She had been through a lot, so he refused to entertain such heat-producing ideas. He had rescued her and made himself responsible for her welfare.

All he wanted to do right now was find the gold. Then whoever else was after it would no longer have any reason to bother Celia. And Morgan, himself, could get the hell out of this crap-filled town.

11

Celia winced slightly as she stretched, then noticed Morgan. "What are you looking so angry about this morning? And you're already up and dressed. Where are you going?"

"Nowhere without you. I'm not leaving you alone."

"I want to go."

"Go where?"

"Anywhere! Out of doors. I want to go outside."

She swung her legs carefully off the edge of the bed and sat up. "The whole time I was held captive, I had this horrible feeling that I'd never see the sky again. I guess I still have it." She nodded eagerly, as if having decided for sure. "I want to go outside."

"I'll take you out, if you're up to it," Morgan assured her. "We'll go to the cafe and have breakfast." He grinned down at her. "But I don't think you can go in your nightgown."

Celia put on the blue print dress that she had worn the first time Morgan had seen her struggling in the clutches of Brant Corson. She managed her clothing, but Morgan helped her with her dainty boots. When she had arranged her auburn hair in its usual becoming style, she took a deep breath, stood somewhat unsteadily at first, and then pronounced herself ready to go.

They made it to the cafe, and Jason limped out of the kitchen to say hello to Morgan and congratulate Celia on her recovery.

"I told him he didn't have to work today," Florrie said. "But he insists he's all right."

After a leisurely breakfast, Celia still wanted to walk some more. So they left the cafe and started up the main street. Morgan enjoyed Celia walking beside him along the plank sidewalk of Lost Canyon. His boots made deep clunking sounds and her dainty ones tap-tapped along beside him.

He vowed again that he wouldn't let her out of his sight until he had dealt with the man who had been responsible for her kidnapping. Even though he was fairly certain now who had ordered her brought back in a trunk, without proof he'd be a fool to openly accuse the fastest gun in town.

Celia had been quiet, apparently thinking, too. "If Hex had told me he needed my help to dispose of stolen gold, I wouldn't have come to help him," she declared.

"I'm glad you did," Morgan told her. "I'm sorry about all the trouble you've gone through, of course." In a moment he added, "There's a reward for anyone who finds the gold, you know. The federal government offers it."

As they strolled along up the main street, Morgan saw Sheriff Tyler coming in the opposite direction. He was walking and talking with Rebecca Petersen. So, Morgan thought, she was still here.

The sheriff stopped in front of them to say

that he was glad to see Miss Fair up and around. "Now you can come to the office with me, and we'll fill out that report before the circuit judge comes in. He should be here in a couple of days."

Celia ignored the sheriff and put out her hand to the woman beside him. "I don't believe we've met, I'm Celia Fair."

Rebecca gave her name, glanced briefly at Morgan, and then said, "Excuse me. I'm going into the church to light a candle."

The church was a few steps back in the direction from which she and the sheriff had come. Morgan had never really noticed the church before, but then he wasn't much of a churchgoer. Churches had more to do with mothers, he'd always thought, than with men.

Celia clung tightly to his hand. "Is that lady upset about something?" she asked.

Morgan's pride told him that Rebecca had looked just a bit jealous. But he wasn't going to tell Celia that.

Before either of them could say more, a man riding fast tore up the street. Stopping just past them, he dashed into the church. Immediately the church bells began to ring.

"What the hell's that for?" Morgan wanted to know, looking up at the steeple. "It's only Saturday."

"Indian attack!" the sheriff shouted and took off at a run in the direction of his office.

A shopkeeper and two customers ran into the street. The nearest saloon emptied.

"Indians! Indians!"

Suddenly there was a sound like thunder a long way off. Hoof beats.

"My God, they're right. Those damned

Washos again!"

Morgan practically dragged Celia to the church. He hustled her up the steps and inside. "Get in here. And stay put until I come back for you."

"Stay with me."

He kissed her quickly. "I'll be back."

More men came out of buildings, loading rifles as they ran and taking cover.

The hoof beats came closer and Morgan could hear the Indians' war cries. He ducked behind the corner of the church as a band of Indians made their first pass. Flaming arrows streaked through the air. The church was made of stone, it would probably not be in danger. The Indians swung left and he could hear them turn down the alley.

A hundred yards away and across the street, the livery stable roof suddenly glowed with flame. Willie, followed by his barking dog, led two horses through the side doors. He slapped their rears and dashed back into the burning barn. In seconds he emerged with two more. One of them was Morgan's bay gelding.

Morgan dashed across the street and made for the barn. Willie turned to go back into the building now engulfed in flames. Morgan threw him aside. He struggled to get back on his feet. "There's one more."

"I'll get him."

In seconds, Morgan returned leading a stallion. Stoneagle's black stallion. With a smack on his flank, he ran off down the field toward the other horses. From the tack room, they managed to save a few saddles.

"Anybody in there? Your pa?" Morgan asked Willie.

Willie shook his head. "Nobody. Pa's down at the Dubloon."

The Indians came down the street again making another pass. Morgan ducked behind a buckboard and dragged Willie with him. Men, rifles blazing, ducked for cover behind wagons or back into doorways.

Burning arrows flew overhead. One embedded itself in the roof of the General Emporium, smoldered for seconds, then the roof burst into flames. These braves sure knew how to make a mess.

An arrow went through a window at the hotel down the street and set curtains afire.

Three more Indians, apparently just arrived, galloped their Pintos across the clearing and into the Main Street, shooting with rifles at anything that moved. With his Bisley Colts Morgan dropped one that got close enough with a bullet into the neck. The Indian screamed, fell from his horse, and a fountain of blood gushed from his jugular.

The others kept coming. Rifle fire exploded from doorways and windows of burning buildings. Indians fell. Some tried to crawl to cover. Few made it.

"They've got guns, Willie. Stay down," Morgan warned. He marveled at the kid's guts.

"Those fire arrows are doing worse than the guns," Willie said. "They're wrecking the town."

Morgan scanned the perimeter of the buildings for some sign of Burning Arrow. He had to be the one behind the attack. But how many braves had joined him? Not the whole tribe, but they moved so fast, it was hard to tell how many there were.

He glanced across the street toward the church. No smoke appeared near the stone structure. So far, Celia was safe.

A brave rounded a corner. Morgan picked him off. His bow, already drawn, skittered an arrow across the dust.

Down at the center of town, about in front of the sheriff's office, a gun battle erupted. Rifles and hand guns blazed from windows. Return fire splintered a door.

Morgan traced the source of the outside shots. Two Indians appeared on the roof of the feed and lumber building pouring lead into the sheriff's office. Morgan's Bisley Colts wouldn't carry that far. But someone's rifle did. One Indian threw up his arms, and he and his rifle toppled from the roof, making a dull permanent thud heard the length of the street as he hit the ground. He didn't move again.

Smoke filled Morgan's eyes. The burning dry wood and hay in the building behind him nearly choked him. He lifted off his Stetson and ducked his head into the nearby watering trough. An arrow missed him by inches.

Morgan wanted to move but scanning the street for the next nearest cover, he found none. Burning buildings needed help, but they could do nothing about that until they got rid of the damned Indians.

Just then Morgan spotted Burning Arrow riding fast. The brave aimed the rifle just as Sheriff Bert Tyler appeared around the side of his office. As Morgan watched fascinated, from his spot behind the big watering trough, wondering which of his enemies would win this match, they both fired. Burning Arrow appeared to dive from his horse. He landed in the dust of the street and his mount thundered on without him.

As suddenly as it had begun, the attack ended. With their leader dead, the braves who were still alive fled. The street became quiet. Nobody moved for two or three long, still minutes.

Willie started to stand up, but Morgan grabbed him and pulled him down again. "May not be over."

The acrid smell of gun fire lay silently on the still air. Smoke billowed straight up, masking the sun, covering the town with an eerie gray pall. In the distance, receding horses' hooves pounded out of town. The attack was over.

Finally the populace came alive. Fire brigades formed. Water was brought to the fires any way they could bring it.

Morgan strode toward the spot where he had seen Burning Arrow fall. As he approached, he saw Tyler go out to Burning Arrow and give the carcass a vicious kick. Morgan heard the sheriff say, "Smart ass, knew too much anyhow."

Morgan pretended not to hear. He glanced around at the bodies, some red skinned, some white.

He joined a bucket brigade putting out the roof fire at the Emporium. It hadn't as good a start as some, so they were able to put it out before damage moved far into the store itself.

The stable and its supply of feed inside were lost, but the horses were safe, thanks to Willie's quick thinking in the beginning. Women, working from inside, had saved the hotel.

When the townsfolk seemed to have things under control again, Morgan hurried back to the church and Celia.

After the cacaphony of the battle, the church

presented extreme quiet. His eyes adjusted to the dimmer interior. Although there was smokey sun shining through the handcrafted, stained glass windows, it took getting used to.

He saw Celia sitting in a pew with her head bowed. As he went into the row, she looked up and smiled. "Oh, I'm so glad you're all right. Is it over? What happened?"

"It's over. We've tangled with Burning Arrow before, but he won't lead braves out to kill white men again."

"Did you shoot him?"

"The sheriff shot him."

They sat in silence for a little while. Morgan thought about the church. It had offered haven for Celia when the attack came. This was a place of sanctuary, topped by the tower with bells that not only called people to worship, but also warned of attack.

"Tower," Morgan said aloud. "Steeple. Spire. It could have been a steeple instead of a tepee."

"What?" Celia obviously couldn't make out what he was talking about.

"The old man, Gramps, left a clue. Jason and I thought the clue meant a tepee. He searched his pockets and found the paper on which he had made the drawing and showed it to her.

"What is it?" Celia frowned at the pencil marks. "I'm sorry, I didn't mean your drawing wasn't . . . nice," she finished lamely.

Morgan laughed at her trying to save his feelings. "It's a crude picture of the clue the old man carved into a log on his cabin. We thought it was a rainbow with an arrow pointing to a tepee."

She nodded. "It's sort of like that."

"But it could be a steeple, the spire of a

church, instead of a tepee."

Celia shrugged. "What is it going to mean, when you decide which it is?"

Morgan grinned at her, glanced around to see whether anyone else was near and smoothing the paper on his knee, said, "If the old man meant it to be a steeple, it could mean that the gold is somewhere in the church, instead of in an Indian tepee."

"Oh, the gold again." Celia sighed.

"If I can find the gold, the others who want it will give up trying to get information from you, information that you obviously don't have."

They sat for another quiet period, gazing around them. As he sat there in the stillness, his mind could see again the poem Hex had written, as Celia had copied it for him.

Open so to see
the book lies on the table
Underneath them all
is the treasure of my fable.

Suddenly Morgan jumped to his feet. "My God, it's right in our laps!"

He pulled Celia by the arm and headed for the front of the church.

On the altar table lay a large open Bible.

They went up the two steps to the altar and Morgan stared down at the Bible. Now here was a book from which came no gunslinging Corsons. Here was an open book on a table.

He took hold of the edges of the table to move it. It seemed to be fastened down. He squatted, examining the base of the table. It was like a cupboard with a small door.

He turned the small wooden hook and opened

the little door. Inside were two shelves, empty
except for offering baskets. What made the
table so heavy?

Celia stood by watching. Morgan glanced up
at her, thinking about the way she had watched
him in his hotel room when he was hiding her
leather case which had contained the note
about the book on the table. He was sure he had
found that table. But how could he get under it?

Morgan felt around the bottom shelf inside
and found two crudely formed, but clever,
sliding catches. He pushed each of them back,
then stood and easily lifted the table. He moved
it to one side.

He knelt again and examined the floor.

"Ha!" He took his knife out of his boot and
carefully sticking the point between two
boards, raised one of them easily. He removed
another board and reached into the space
between the floor and the foundation rock. In a
moment his hand touched metal. His heart
thumped faster. He knew what it had to be.

He felt the size and shape of the cool metal he
had encountered. He grasped it and withdrew a
ten-pound gold bar.

Before he could reach in and bring out
another, a thundrous voice froze them where
they were.

"Knew damn well some son-of-a-bitch would
lead me to it if I waited around this hellhole
long enough." Sheriff Bert Tyler stood in the
center aisle with a forty-four trained on
Morgan. "Just go ahead and lift the other ones
out of there. How many are there? Four?"

Keeping his eyes riveted on Tyler, Morgan
reached slowly into the hole and removed
another bar and, with great deliberation, set it

on the floor. Then he carefully brought up a third. His mind raced trying to get an idea of how to get out of this with his life, if not the gold.

He pulled out the fourth bar and set it beside the others. "All yours, Sheriff, we were about to come and call you. You'll want to get in touch with the Federal Government."

"Sure, Morgan." The sheriff took a couple of steps closer. "I'll want to get in touch with the fuckin' undertaker, is who I'll want to get in touch with. Better draw out your old Colts there, so it will look as if I shot you in the process of robbing the church."

Morgan wondered whether there was a way he could draw and shoot without getting either Celia or himself shot up too badly. "Well, if that's the plan, Sheriff, this young lady had better get down out of the line of fire."

"Don't think that's necessary, you're both off to the happy hunting grounds along with that stupid brave I just took care of outside. Now take out your weapon, carefully. You can lay it down on the floor, there. So's it'll look like that's where it fell."

Morgan put his hand on the top of the Bisley. He knew he couldn't draw. He didn't know how long he could stall this lunatic in front of him before it would be over.

Suddenly another voice rang out in the house of worship. "No, Bert Tyler, that's not the plan after all."

The sheriff whirled to look at Rebecca Petersen who stood between rows of the back pews holding a large bore pistol in both hands. It was pointed at the sheriff.

Morgan drew and fired. At the same instant,

Rebecca discharged her oversized weapon. The kick of the heavy piece set her backward hard onto the seat.

Blood ran from the sheriff's head completely obscuring his features. Torrents of blood spurted from his chest as if pumped directly out by his heart. The sheriff's gun arm swung down, and he collapsed by degrees. It seemed as if all motion was suspended on a string of beaded movements. The sheriff's knees buckled, his head sagged, his rump reached the floor first, then his back and shoulders and head.

"You got my man killed," Rebecca said. "You're not going to get his gold." She spoke more softly now. "I'm claiming a share of that gold, folks." She sat there and reloaded the old pistol and slid it back into her reticule.

Celia Fair had not screamed, nor had she fainted. She stared first at Rebecca, watching until the gun was safely tucked away. Then she turned her attention to the downed sheriff. After another moment, she looked at Morgan and smiled, as if something nice had just happened.

People began to come into the church, "What were the shots?" "Who shot the sheriff?"

"Lots of folks told him he should resign." It was the liveryman's voice, Willie's father.

Jason limped up the side aisle and came to Morgan's side. "You all right?" He looked at the sheriff, then stared down at the bars by Morgan's feet. "You found it!" He waited a long moment then asked, "Now what?"

Rebecca Petersen picked her way carefully through the group of people beginning to clog the center aisle. Some of them had probably come to give thanks for their survival after the Indian raid. Others wanted to know what the gun play in the church was all about.

"He was a bad man," Rebecca announced, standing in the pulpit as if ready to give a sermon.

Everyone stopped moving and talking. Every eye turned toward Rebecca.

Rebecca pointed down at the sheriff. "This man was going to kill two people, to keep them from giving that gold . . ." Again she pointed. ". . . to the Federal Government of this country. He planned to tell the people of this town that he had caught them robbing your church. A criminal hid the gold in there and now it has been found. The reward will be divided among those who found it." She moved away from the pulpit and stood beside Jason and the other two on the raised platform.

Morgan finally answered Jason Isley's question. "Now what? I'll tell you what." Picking up the gold bars, he handed Jason one. "Comes out just right. One for you. One for Celia. One for Rebecca. And one for me."

The undertaker came and had his men carry Sheriff Bert Tyler's remains away. No one seemed distressed about that.

The minister of the church was heard to remark that he had never drawn such a crowd on his best Sunday.

One man kept saying that he thought Lee Morgan would be a good sheriff.

Morgan stepped down and tapped him on the shoulder. "There's your man, if you want an honest, hard-working, land-owner for sheriff of Lost Canyon." He pointed to Jason Isley.

Celia told Jason they would telegraph her

U.S. senator and tell him the gold had been found.

Morgan dropped a light kiss on Celia's cheek. "Tell him *part* of the gold has been found." He took a last look at her and strode out of the church.

Her gold bar wrapped in a kerchief, Rebecca Peterson hurried after Morgan.

When Rebecca knocked on his door, Morgan was just ready to leave. By her costume, he would have taken her for a young boy, except for her awesome bosom.

"Did I hear you mutter something about San Diego?" she asked him.

Morgan nodded. "With a horse, and a canteen, you can make it. I plan to send young Willie a black snake whip from down there. I also understand you can get rid of most anything of value in San Diego."